Dear Rick

Thank you for your friendship and your interest in my writing.

Lois

The Tree in the Meadow: The Adventures of Toby and Tish
An autobiographical novel by L. E. Ricker Schofield

ISBN   978-0-578-74383-7

Printed in the United States of America
2020

In some instances, any resemblance to persons living or dead is purely coincidental.

# ACKNOWLEDGMENT

A special thankyou to my son-in-law, David Maurer, my computer guru and biggest fan, who has spent hours of his free time formatting my book and readying it for publication.

## Also by L. E. Ricker Schofield

*61 Threadneedle Street*

# THE TREE IN THE MEADOW:

## The Adventures of Toby and Tish

## L. E. RICKER SCHOFIELD

I dedicate this book to my loving Mom and Dad, who taught me the rewards of hard work, the joys of leisure, right from wrong, contentment and the notion that one's freedom requires self-discipline and responsibility

*Mom and Dad - 1924*

*Tish & Toby*

# 1

## The Big Surprise

I usually liked making soda, especially the first batch of the season, but it was too hot that day to wash and scald bottles. I'd set up my wash and rinse tubs on the cement bench Uncle Edgar'd made. Although it was well shaded by the huge sugar maple, the same sprawling sugar maple that shaded my bedroom window, it didn't help. I was hot, sticky, and I dreaded it every time a car went by our house churning up a cloud of dust. With the slightest westerly breeze, it drifted my way and sifted through the screens settling on everything I'd just dusted.

Ours was a typical, old farmhouse, white clapboard bottom, green-shingled top. It was situated on a knoll about fifty feet off the main road (which you know by now was unpaved). A long driveway running easterly led to the barn and the sawmill. The dug well, also on the north side, could be seen from the kitchen windows. The outhouse, hidden by a row of giant pines on the south side, was a two-seater, but for the life of me, I couldn't imagine why, since only one person at a time used it. Beyond the lawn and the driveway for a mile in either direction, were the orchards, hay fields and gardens.

Mom glanced in my direction but said nothing as she came from the kitchen to the screened porch to add a bottle of birch beer extract to the cannerful of water, sugar and yeast heating on the kerosene stove. We'd retrieved this old relic from the dump to use on the porch during hot spells. It caught fire now and then, but we always managed to cart it outside in time to prevent a catastrophe.

"Almost finished," I offered. I stopped thinking about how uncomfortable I was and got back to work.

From force of habit Mom lived life by the calendar. Wash

on Monday. Iron on Tuesday. Plant peas by St. Patrick's Day,
and God forbid, don't wear white shoes or take off your undershirt,
no matter how hot it gets, before Decoration Day. So, you see, that
was my problem. Decoration Day was still two weeks away. I
was itchy and sweaty, but I couldn't complain to Mom because she
wasn't talking to me.

"It's just her way," Dad would always say. "A woman has
her quiet times, and we must be patient." I didn't really understand
and wouldn't dream of asking a personal question, so I endured the
long periods of silence with my Dad.

The soda cases were heavy, but I managed to lug them to the
porch. Bottling and capping were fun. I'd just finished the last
one and was about to store the batch behind the kitchen stove to
"work" when I heard Dad's old International® chugging up the
driveway. Mom rushed past me, and I followed with a sickening
feeling in the pit of my stomach. Dad never left the woods with
only half a jag of wood unless he'd cut himself with the ax or
something dreadful like that.

"I'm all right," he called, reading our thoughts and

expressions. "I came home early because I found a pet for Tish." He grinned broadly, holding a toothpick tight between his teeth in the right-hand corner of his mouth as he always did. "You'll never guess what I've got for you this time, young lady," he teased.

"Bet I can," I ventured, my eyes wide with excitement. "A baby bird. A bunny. I know, a raccoon. A *skunk*? Come on Dad, SHOW ME!"

Dad shook his head from side to side as he stepped backward out of the cab to the running board with the surprise in his arms. His blue work shirt, striped with salt and sweat stains, stuck to his back.

"A BABY FAWN," I screamed. "A new-born baby fawn. I've never seen one so small or so closeup." His silky, cinnamon-colored fur was covered with a zillion white spots. "I can't believe it! A baby deer! Is it a doe or a buck?"

"A buck," Dad replied, beaming from ear to ear. He put him in my arms, and I pressed him close to me. He nuzzled his nose in my ear and made a funny noise.

"Sounds like the little fella's hungry, Tish, and those lanky legs of his could use a little stretching, too. Remember, he's been cooped up in the truck for quite some time."

Dad and I sat down in the grass with the fawn between us. Mom came too, but she didn't sit, just stood and watched, never saying a word. I felt guilty feeling so happy, but I couldn't help it. I was bursting.

"What're you going to call him?" Dad asked.

"His name's Toby," I answered without the slightest bit of hesitation.

"Toby and Tish. Now that's a pair!"

"He's so little. Did he wander away from his mother and get lost?"

"No. When I felled a white ash this morning, I think a branch probably grazed him and stunned him a bit. I saw a doe and one fawn hightail it out of there, but she left this one behind. I knew she wouldn't come back for him, so I figured...."

Before he could finish, I threw my arms around his neck and hugged him, sweat and all. The tears came, as they always did. I was so emotional that it was disgusting. I was going to have to work on that. I was sure nobody in eighth grade cried over everything.

"You'll need a bottle and nipple to feed that animal," Mom said out of the blue. "If I'm going to get to town before Mr. Morris' store closes, I'd better get a move on."

Dad winked at me, and I heard him utter a sigh of relief.

"Gee, thanks, Mom. I'll start supper while you're gone."

"I suppose you're going to want that deer to sleep on the porch tonight. I want you to fix him a box and then peel the potatoes. And don't forget the soda. You've got to put that away, too."

With that, she took off her apron, got her pocketbook and everyday hat and waved goodbye, just as though nothing was ever wrong.

*Gram*

## 2

## Decoration Day

A small branch from the huge maple brushed the screen in my bedroom window pestering me to wake up. I rolled over away from the nagging sound and sifted daylight and tried to dose. I drifted off again until a rooster crowed, heralding a new day with his annoying alarm. He kept it up until I obediently arose and through squinty eyes blew out the flame still burning in my night lamp. As I did, glimpses of Toby and the weekend's excitement returned.

Being a typical twelve-year-old going on thirteen, I usually primped on a school morning, combing the dark eyebrows I wasn't allowed to pluck yet and rubbing the glossless lips that wouldn't see lipstick for another year, but not this morning. I yanked a brush through my dirty blond hair, gave it a few quick strokes, wound up a few clothespin curlers haphazardly around the edges and tiptoed down the creaky stairs to see my new pet.

I took the pitcher of milk from the ice box. A good five inches of cream had settled on the top overnight, so I shook it well before filling Toby's bottle and putting it on the kerosene stove to heat.

"Hi, little one," I said, lifting him out of his box and cradling him in my arms. "Let's go exploring until your breakfast is ready." I sat Indian fashion in the grass, setting Toby free to investigate. His first discovery was a patch of tiger lilies, a flourishing spot dampened by tubs of wash water. Unfortunately, it was also perfect for black snakes. As one slithered within inches of his inquisitive nose, he backed away and headed in my direction as fast as his wobbly legs would carry him.

"Don't be afraid, pumpkin," I reassured him. "It's only an

ugly old black snake, creepy but harmless." I rubbed his silky coat with my cheek and closed my eyes. "I still can't believe you're really mine to raise."

Toby responded by nuzzling his nose in my ear and making that funny noise again. I took it to mean that he was ready for his bottle. He nursed until his sides bulged and was satisfied.

Mom was up and had a fire blazing and coffee perking when I went inside. The aroma of coffee and the tantalizing smell of hickory-smoked bacon intermingled, and suddenly I realized that I was hungry too. She finished cutting another slice from the slab before wrapping it carefully in waxed paper.

Testing her mood, I gave her a peck on the cheek as I snitched a rasher of crisp bacon from the pile draining on a piece of brown paper on the warming shelf above the stove. She slapped my hand affectionately, and I knew things were back to normal.

"Stop picking and sit down and eat before you're late and miss the bus," she said as she fastened a thermos of Ovaltine® in my lunch box.

That's what I wanted to talk to you about, Mom. *Please* let me stay home, just today."

"You sick again?" she asked, coming over to feel my head.

"No, but I will be if anything happens to Toby while I'm away. He's not used to his surroundings yet, and besides, he needs to be fed every few hours."

"You know how your father feels about truancy. He'd agree that you can't afford to miss one more day of school this year. I'll feed that deer of yours and keep an eye on him while I do the wash."

Washday in Stonetown was an all-day affair, with backyards lined with flapping, white sheets and threadbare dishtowels. No wonder they wore out. After cooking them in a copper boiler, they were washed, bleached and blued.

"But when Dad was a boy," I argued, unwilling to give up so easily, "his father kept him home any time he needed him on the farm."

"Things are different now."

"All right," I sighed, knowing when I was licked. "But is it okay to invite Mim to spend the Decoration Day weekend with us?

I can't wait 'til she sees Toby."

"Fine with me, *if* you two stay out of trouble."

"Hurray!" I shouted in a somewhat muffled tone.

"Don't talk with your mouth full."

"Thanks for everything, Mom," I said after I finished my roll and butter and washed it down with the rest of my milk. "She'll love Toby. We'll be good," I added with a grin.

"Ah huh. I've heard that song before." She raised her eyebrows and pursed her lips into a smile.

My best friend, Mim, was as fond of animals as I was, but she couldn't have a pet because her older sister was allergic. Her folks were rich. They had electricity, indoor plumbing and a telephone. The *trouble* we got into the last time I stayed at her house for the weekend was this: Early one morning we heard a stray kitten meowing. We sneaked outside, found it and brought it back to bed with us. It was a real cutie pie. We couldn't tell exactly what color it was until we cleaned it with dry shampoo, the stuff her sister used when she wasn't allowed to wash her hair. Neither of us thought it was so adorable the following week when we both ended up at Dr. Graham's with ring worm. It took forever and several bottles of chalky pink gook to get rid of it.

"The time is now 7:30," the radio announcer stated as if he were my own personal prodder.

"Good grief," I exclaimed, staring at the radio. "I've only got ten minutes to get dressed." I bolted up the stairs deciding what I would wear. Choices were few since I could only buy three school dresses a year. Lucky for me, though, I sewed (*well, so-so*) and had just made a dirndl out of three blue-printed feed sacks.

We had to take sewing and cooking from fifth through eighth grades. Our teacher was a real fussbudget. Every stitch had to be just so or you had to rip it out. Mim did okay, but I didn't have a lot of patience for it. I was really dreading next year when we had to make our own graduation dresses.

Miss Crocker would die if she knew I stitched the seams of my dirndl without basting first, I thought, as I whisked my skirt from around the broom handle. I slipped last year's birthday blouse over my dumb undershirt, slid into my anklets and loafers and threw the clothespins in the general direction of my dresser before Mom yelled, "BUS!"

Like a Blondie and Dagwood movie, I grabbed my lunch box from her as I flew out of the door.

\*\*\*\*

Mim's bus pulled in just ahead of mine. "You might know she'd be on bus patrol today," I grumbled, "just when I have so much to tell her." I stood aside out of the confusion trying to be patient. She finally noticed me and grinned. "Hurry up," I mouthed. She made a face and returned to her serious pose.

"Walk," she warned. Her green eyes, even greener in the sunlight, made a sharp contrast to the black mop of curls that framed her face. *She's gorgeous, I thought. Maybe I should cut my hair too, I pondered,* springing a spiraling curl, shaped like a clothespin, until it fell softly over the slight rise of my blouse. *Nope. I ain't. Laura says David likes girls with long hair.*

"What's the story, morning-glory?" Mim kidded in her best May West fashion after her last charge had alighted safely.

"Be serious, would ya, Mim?"

"Okay. But tell me. What's all this about? Did you get a

note from David?"

"No. Nothing like that. Dad found a baby deer in the woods, and I'm going to raise him," I blurted out.

"You're kidding! Lucky you," Mim squealed, locking arms at the shoulders and taking me round and round. "When will I get to see him?"

"How about spending Decoration Day weekend at my house?"

"Gee, thanks, but I don't think I should with your Mom in one of her silent moods."

"Oh, that is my other good news. Mom's talking to us again."

"That's wonderful, Tish. In that case I'd love to come."

I was fidgety all through arithmetic, history, English and art. Luckily, at two o'clock a meeting was called for seventh-grade girls who wanted to be garland bearers at graduation. Mim, Laurie, Sally and I were the first ones in the auditorium.

"Form two rows, now, girls, according to height, tallest last," Miss Somers ordered as soon as everyone arrived. Some squabbling erupted as friends were separated. At least Sally and I were together. Poor Mim and Laurie got stuck with Jan and Shirley. They were nice, but they wore nylon stockings, lipstick, and plucked their eyebrows already, much too old-acting for us.

"Let's reassemble in the hall, girls, and practice coming in to the music.

Mrs. Barnes began to play Mendelssohn's "Spring Song", and I got goose pimples. It was so beautiful that I got emotional, of course. Classical music was familiar to me, because Mom had insisted that I take piano lessons when I started second grade. "Da..da da da Da! Da! Da! da da.. da da.. da da.. da da.." I hummed.

Partners, keep pace so that the ribbons are even."

I closed my eyes and imagined David walking down the aisle to "Melody in F". Gosh, would he be handsome in his white ducks and blue blazer.

"That's fine, girls. We'll practice again in a few weeks with the graduates and their flower girls and boys."

The dismissal bell rang, and everyone scattered to catch a different bus, shouting their good-byes on the run.

The hour-long bus ride seemed endless, but finally Ben Kirby got off, and my stop was next, thank heavens. Would Toby be waiting for me or not? Had he wondered away and gotten lost? I barreled into the yard expecting the worst, but there he was, sunning himself in the grass while Mom and Gram folded the laundry and put it neatly into a huge, wicker clothes basket.

"Your mother's either awful clean or awful dirty," Gram joked to me.

I'd heard that quip at least a hundred times before, so I smiled, kissed them hello and flopped down beside Toby. "How've you been today all by yourself, my little dumpling?" I asked, snuggling next to him and kissing his satiny-smooth ears.

"He's been good as gold, the little angel," Gram answered. "I swear, Letitia, you could tame a wildcat if you tried." (Gram called me by my proper name, since I was named after her. Everyone else called me Tish).

I loved Gram. She came from Ireland to the New Country at twenty-five, following in the footsteps of her older brothers and sisters. She boasted often of her five crossings. It took courage to continue her final journey after the ship sprang a leak midway and had to return to port.  Gram was as neat and clean as my mother's wash.  Her long, gray hair was pulled back severely from her unblemished face into a crisscross bun, except when she went to bed.  Then she braided it into a thick pigtail that fell to her waist.  Life wasn't easy for her, but she never complained.  She grew a whole field of gladiolas and sold them at the lakes to pay her taxes.  I idolized her because she was so thoughtful.  For instance, Mom's birthday was in early March, long before the forsythia bloomed.  She'd pick a bunch of it in February, keep it in a bucket of water next to the wood stove and have it flowering in time for Mom's tea party every year.

"Go change, Tish, before you get grass stains on your skirt," Mom said wearily, taking the last pair of Dad's overalls from the line.

"Okay, Mom.    But look, ain't he adorable?"

"He's cute, all right, Letitia, but remember, kittens become cats."

I sloughed off Gram's remark and changed the subject.

"Are you coming to our picnic Decoration Day?"

"With bells on.   Can't wait to try that birch beer I hear you made."

"Tish!" Mom snapped.

"I'm going."

****

May 30th fell on a Monday, so Mim and I had two glorious days to devote to Toby.

"It's my turn to feed him," said Mim.

"Go to it."

"Gosh, he's famished."   Toby had gotten much stronger over the last couple of weeks.   He sucked so hard that the nipple came off, and warm milk sprayed all over his face.   Mim laughed hysterically, throwing herself into a pile of hay and holding her stomach.

"You little guzzler," I scolded, wiping him off with my shirt. "Don't worry.   There's more where this came from."

"It's your turn now," said Mim still giggling.

A pickup truck pulled up the driveway and stopped down by

the house. I recognized it as the game warden's. He always showed up when you least expected him, trying to surprise a poacher most times. Dad talked to him for a few minutes and he left.

The day was so beautiful that Dad decided to work in the woods a couple of hours before the parade, over Mom's objections, of course. Mim and I washed our hair with water from the rain barrel and took turns taking baths in a big wash tub in the kitchen. Then wrapped in chenille robes, we ran upstairs to dress.

"Hurray!" I yelled. "No more stupid undershirts."

"To the cedar chest with you all," Mim playacted as she took each one from my drawer on the end of my baton and dropped it disdainfully into the chest.

"You clown," I chuckled. "Get dressed."

Meanwhile, I slipped into my new organdy dress. "Well, what do you think?" I asked, striking a model's pose. "It's got to double for graduation."

"Wow! Wait 'til David sees you in that."

"I've decided that the only way to impress David is to hit a home run during recess."

"Now, now.  Artie thinks David might ask you to the eighth-grade dance."

"Seeing's believing.  I don't think I'll hold my breath until he does.  My, don't you look patriotic in your red, white and blue."

Never missing a cue, Mim picked up a flag laying on my bed and, to the tune of "She's a Grand Olde Flag," marched down the stairs and outside singing.  We took turns pushing each other on the swing under the maple tree as we continued our serenade.  I knew the alto to "Now is the Hour", so we sang it over and over trying to perfect the harmony.  After the umpteenth time I got sick of it. "Boy, Dad's late.  I bet Mom's mad."

"I'm not mad," Mom said from the porch.  "I'm worried. I'll take the car and go look for him if he doesn't come soon."

With that, Dad staggered around the corner of the house, holding a bloody towel to his head.  Blood ran down his face, and his blue overalls were saturated.

"My God, Wes, what happened?  I didn't hear the truck."

"I walked.  Luke borrowed my truck to fetch…."

"Tish!  Quick!  Get clean towels.  MOVE!  We've got to

get him to the doctor fast."

Dad was chalk white when we got him in the car. Mim and I got in the back.

"Keep that towel good 'n tight, you hear girls?" Mom ordered, her voice shaking.

"The ax bounced off a knot and hit me in the head," Dad tried to explain.

"Don't talk, Wes. Save your strength."

Down the bumpy road we flew, leaving a trail of dust a mile long behind us. Once we reached the paved road, it was clear sailing to Dr. Graham's house. Before the car even came to a complete stop, Mom snapped, "Mim, RUN. See if he's in."

Mim dashed to the door and pounded on it. "Dr. Graham, Dr. Graham," she called as loud as she could. "Please answer. It's an emergency!"

The house was silent.

"Get in," Mom shouted, her voice and hands now shaking. Mom was panicking, and I knew why. One road connected this town to the next, and the parade had already begun. Dad leaned his head back against the seat.   He was weakening quickly.

We all strained to hear the first drumbeat.   Rata-tat-tat, rata-tat-tat, rata-tat-tat.   Mom pulled to the side and stopped.   "Tish, let Mim hold the towel and you go ride on the front fender.   Tell the marchers to let us through, because this is an emergency.   Hold onto the headlight, you hear?"

"I'll do it," Mim offered.

"No.   Tish rides like this almost every Sunday night when she and Dad ride through the hayfield in the dark to spot deer."   Then Mom turned on the headlights and crawled along with her hand resting on the horn.

Spectators dressed in their Sunday best lined the street on both sides with flags in hand, eyes right.   As the distance between us and the parade narrowed, Mom hit the horn and all eyes turned left.

"Tish!   What in the world?"   Mim's Mother and Father's voices trailed off as we were swallowed by the oncoming bands, veterans and politicians.

"Please move.   We've got to get to a doctor," Tish pleaded, with tears streaming down her face." All of a sudden, the bands stopped playing, and the marchers peeled aside to let us through. It was truly amazing.

We reached Dr. Skinner's office in the nick of time, because Dad collapsed on the floor unconscious the minute we got him into the office.

****

Our picnic was mighty quiet that afternoon. We'd all had quite enough excitement for one day. After Mim's parents came and took her home, we carried Dad's Morris chair outside so he could be cool and comfortable under the big maple.

"Tish." Dad's voice was unnaturally thin and frail.

"Yes, Dad," I replied, smoothing his rough, calloused hand with my fingers.

"Where was Toby this afternoon?"

"I put him in the chicken run before I got dressed for the parade. Why?"

"The game warden was around and says you can't keep him."

"What do you mean, I can't keep him? Is that what Sly told you when he came snooping around here yesterday?"

Dad squeezed my hand. "Simmer down, young lady. Let's be fair. He's only doing his job. The law says you can't keep a wild animal penned up and that's that."

"All right. I won't pen him up anymore. There's no need to anyhow. Ask Mom. When I'm at school he roams in the woods for a while and then comes right back in time to meet me at the bus. I plan to spend my whole summer vacation exploring with him. By the time fall comes, he'll know our property backwards and forwards."

"That's all well and good, but don't forget you'll be working at the lake one day a week, and what about your week's vacation at Mim's house?"

"I'll handle it. You'll see. Ain't Mim welcome here?"

"Of course she is."

"Well, then, it's settled. She'll come here instead."

*Tish and Star*

# 3

## The Bitter With The Better

By the time school was out, Dad's head had healed, but the scar was a doozie, not as bad as some of his others, though, especially the one up the center of his thumb or the one across his big toe. Those gave me the willies. When it came time to have the stitches removed, Dad was too busy to go back to the doctor, so he had Mom take them out. In my book he was the bravest and toughest person I knew, but in this case it was a tossup.

Toby outgrew his box on the porch. I was glad, because although Sly hadn't been around lately, you never knew when he'd show up. I piled a lot of dry hay in a far corner of the lean-to on the east side of the barn for a bed.   This way he was protected from

the weather, yet he was free to come and go as he pleased, which

kept me out of trouble with the law.

For about a month now, every spare minute, after school and

weekends, Toby and I roamed and explored the many acres that

made up our Daisy Meadow Farm.   There was no end to work,

which meant that free time was as scarce as hen's teeth.   Besides

my regular chores like feeding the chickens and gathering the eggs,

pitching hay down from the loft to feed the livestock, hauling water

from the well and scrubbing the kitchen floor, Dad gave me a new

responsibility to add to my list.

Out of the blue a wood customer stopped by and paid off his

bill with a young, black and white Holstein.   She was marked like

a marble cake with a patch of white frosting shaped exactly like a

star right between her eyes.   That made naming her the easiest part

of the deal.   I really didn't mind, because I'd coaxed Dad for a calf

of my own for ages, but Star was a little more than I'd bargained for,

and the timing was downright inconvenient.   Dad warned me that

she didn't cotton to strangers milking her, and, as usual, he was telling the God's honest truth.

"Sorry to have to pile more of a load on your shoulders, Tish," Dad apologized as we walked to the barn with our milk pails.

"It doesn't matter. It's as true as I'm telling you. How many fireplaces and stonewalls are you going to build this summer anyhow?"

"Two of each. They're running me ragged, but as they say, you've got to make hay while the sun shines. Until we see just how ornery this critter is, I'd better milk her and you take Bell."

"No," I objected. "We've got to make friends sooner or later."

"All right. But remember, the secret is to let her know who's boss," Dad said emphatically.

Seconds after I sat down on the milking stool, I knew I should have listened to Dad. Before I got one squirt in the bucket, she kicked her back leg and sent me, the stool and the pail head over teacup into the sawdust.

"You hurt, Tish?" Dad asked, putting his pail down at a safe distance and coming to my rescue.

"I think I just found out who's the boss," I said with a laugh, brushing myself off.  Star turned her head in her stanchion to gloat, bellowing a loud, defiant moo.

"Ready to trade?" Dad asked, half in fun and full in earnest.

"No," I replied stubbornly.  "I just need to think of a way to outsmart her."  I went around and pitched a forkful of hay in her trough, hoping she'd take my bait.  She did, and the duel was over.

There was nothing Toby liked more than raw milk, warm and fresh from the cow, so I wasn't surprised to find him waiting for a bottleful when I finished.  He followed me to the house like a duckling trailing its mother.

Mom was already straining Dad's pail of milk through a cloth into a ten-quart aluminum pot that was in the sink.  Toby followed me right in, and for some reason, Mom didn't object.  I got a loaf of bread from the breadbox, some fixings from the closet and made us up some sandwiches for today's jaunt.

"Are you two rapscallions planning to go traipsing off again all afternoon?  Where in heaven's name do you go anyhow?  I worry about you."

"We ain't playing, Mom. Honest. We're learning everything there is to know about our property, where the caves are, the best fishing holes and the biggest huckleberries. Did you know there's a spring bubbling right out of a rock on this side of Board Mountain?"

"No, I didn't, but remember to tell your dad about that tonight. He's been looking for a spring to tap to bring another vein of water to the barn well." She worked as she talked, filling each sterile bottle carefully and putting a cardboard cap on each one. "Speaking of playing," Mom went on, "you're neglecting your piano practicing by spending so much time with Toby. Mrs. Puffer told me she wants you to learn that big piece. What's it again?"

"Chopin's Polonaise."

"That's it. She wants you to play it by heart for your graduation."

"I know. But I've got a whole year to work on it. Besides, this is my vacation."

"No excuses, young lady. You hear? Make time. Fifteen minutes of Hanons won't kill you, and they'll keep your fingers limber."

It was lucky for me that Mom had her back to me and didn't see the sour face I made.  But what the hay, with a whole glorious summer ahead of us, fifteen minutes a day of unpleasantness seemed bearable.

While I was mulling this over in my mind, deciding where I could fit one more item on my list, Mom let out a yelp.  "What in tarnation?" she cried.

I looked up and saw Mom slapping at Toby's nose, while *my* milk that she was straining gushed and gurgled down the sink. Now I suddenly realized why she hadn't objected to Toby being in the kitchen.  She didn't know he was there!"

"Where's my *fly* swatter?"

It was a slow, deliberate question, with emphasis on the word "fly".  Toby and I didn't wait around long enough to help find it, because I knew she didn't want it to swat flies.  We got out while the getting was good and took cover in the barn until things simmered down.

About nine o'clock I heard the screen door bang.  I opened

the barn door on a crack and peeked out.   Mom was heading for the

Chevy in an awful sweat.

"Shoo," she snarled, whisking our ten lazy cats off the

walkway with her huge pocketbook.   I knew her next words by

heart, because I'd heard them so often.   "The next time the feed

man comes around, I'm going to give you all away."   He'd say,

"Which ones do you want me to take?"   She'd say, "Well, you can't

have Patty or Gus or Henrietta... I guess you can't have any of

them."

"Phew!   It's all clear, Toby.   I wiped the sweat off my

forehead with the back of my hand.   "I'm parched," I said to him.

"How about a cold drink before we tackle the weeding?"

We raced down the stony drive to the well, a thirty-two-foot

hole in the ground, shored up with big, thick rocks to keep the water

icy cold.   For safety's sake it was enclosed by a pitched-roof

wellhouse, screened around the middle to let in the light.   The water

level stayed at six feet, so Dad said, but during a drought, we were

lucky if it stayed at three.

I could draw a bucket of water with my eyes closed:   let the rope down nice and easy over the pulley until you heard the pail splash, wait until you feel it sinking, then heave it up.  Simple as one, two, three.

"Best water in seven states," I told Toby, tipping the bucket to drink but letting a stream of it run down the front of my shirt. "Boy, that feels heavenly," I said, shivering from the shock.  I poured some over Toby's nose to cool him down, and he scampered away kicking up his heels.

I checked the thermometer outside the kitchen window behind me and gave a whistle.  It read 85 degrees in the shade already.  "This is going to be a scorcher," I called to Toby.  "Come on.  I've got to get those beets and carrots weeded before the sun gets higher and I get burned to a crisp."

By eleven, when the weeding I despised was done, my face was beet red from the heat.  The only thing that kept me inching toward the end of the row of carrots was the thought of diving into the old swimming hole afterwards.

Toby was in the doghouse.  He lay supervising me from under the giant, white pines that edged this section of the garden.

Before we made up, I went back to the scene of the crime to cover any telltale hoof prints and to see how many tender, juicy carrot tops he devoured before I caught him. Ruining crops was serious business and not to be taken lightly. Keeping Toby out of a venison stew was going to be a full-time job. I could see it coming.

'Let's go, buddy," I hollered. "No noticeable harm done"

As soon as my eyes adjusted to the darkness of the kitchen (Mom had pulled the shades down to keep it cool), I noticed a note propped against the sugar bowl. It read:

Tish,

1. Watch out for snakes.

2. Swim where you can touch bottom.

3. Be home by 4:00 p.m. Dad needs a hand loading wood.

P.S. I've gone to town to get a permanent wave.

Maybe we won't get a walloping after all, I thought. This note was a sure sign that Mom was willing to let bygones be bygones. After seeing her leave in such a huff, I was certain she was on a rampage. Looking around to see if there was something thoughtful I could do for her before we left, I noticed a trickle of water darkening the cement floor on the porch in front of the ice box. I slid the ice pan out carefully, flinging the water into the yard. Mom would be pleased that I used my head for more than a hat rack (one of her favorite expressions), and it might put us back in her good graces. I scribbled her a quick note telling her where we were going, got into my bathing suit and off we went.

We walked the road a ways, then cut down through the pasture to the path that led to the brook. The overgrown rhododendron formed an arbor overhead, blocking out the sun and keeping the earth damp and cool underfoot. Like coming out of a dark tunnel, we burst into the sunlight again a hop, skip and a jump from the water's edge.

I dove in, not appreciating the natural beauty of the spot but taking it all for granted. A hedgerow of delicate pink mountain laurel hemmed in the opposite shore, while to my right foamy rapids bubbled over skin-smooth rocks into the pool below. I was like a water rat, never getting enough. I fooled around lathering my hair up, piling it high on my head until I looked like a blonde Carmen

Miranda.    Mostly, I swam underwater, relishing its coolness,

surfacing only long enough to take another breath.    Soon, when my

hands got all wrinkly and my teeth chattered, I had to admit that I

was waterlogged and called it quits.    I skipped a couple of stones

that were causing me discomfort across the pond and leveled a few

lumpy places before stretching out on my towel to rest.    I closed my

eyes and listened.    The sounds around me were as soothing as a

symphony.    The sparrows, larks and wrens piped their different

tunes, accompanied by the frogs and a lonely woodpecker.

Since school ended Toby occupied my spare time and my

thoughts.    Relaxing here, though, I thought about David, my first

date and my first corsage that he made from a cluster of delicate,

white lilies of the valley surrounded by wild, blue cornflowers,

pressed between the pages of our "D" encyclopedia.    Mim was

faithful.    She'd written.    Everything she'd suggested sounded like

oodles of fun, especially the moonlight swim.    If David invited one

of the summer girls, I would understand, but to be honest, I would

be crushed.    I lived in another world with no telephone to connect

the two.

Something wet tickled my arm startling me. Mom's first item of business on my shopping list of do's and don'ts came quickly to mind. "Hey, pumpkin," I said to Toby, putting my arm around him. "You scared the dickens out of me."

He stared back innocently.

"Your eyes are gorgeous," I told him. "They remind me of my prize amber aggie, the one I've saved in my Pt. Pleasant jewelry box." His fur stuck to my arm as I drew away, and suddenly I got a spur-of-the-moment idea. "How about taking a dip? Swimming makes you feel like a million." I laughed, remembering Mim's comeback and said aloud, "Yeah, all green and wrinkled."

Picking up my little spindle-legged charge, I waded out waist deep before I let him go, pointing him toward the shore. "Go, Toby, go!" I cheered, clapping my hands. To my surprise he swam like a pro, like he'd been practicing for a coon's age. "Toby," I said proudly, "you're the berries." I draped him with my towel and rubbed him dry.

My stomach told me it was lunchtime, so I slipped my shorts and shirt over my bathing suit, and we moseyed upstream toward our secret spot. I hopped the rocks, missing now and then, while Toby, skirted the edge, amusing himself by nuzzling a wary turtle or sniffing majestic lady slippers or jack-in-the-pulpits along the bank.

We passed under the rotting, wooden bridge a stone's throw away from our destination. At this point the brook widened slightly as it arched around the bend, following the zigzag shape of the mountain. Its flow was sluggish here, allowing for quiet pools to form and fish to hide. A stately pine occupied the point and provided a soft, spongy bed of needles.

I spread my towel and flopped on my stomach to take a long, cold drink before attempting to down one of the peanut butter and jelly sandwiches I'd brought. Toby followed suit, snorting and sneezing as the water went up his nose.

"So, you're getting too big for your britches, are you," I said in a motherly fashion. "All right, little shot, let's learn to drink." With one hand I gently forced his head to the water. I submerged my other hand and put one finger into his mouth. "It shouldn't be any different than weaning a baby calf," I said to myself. Sure enough.  He began to suck, and before I knew it he was drinking on his own.  He was pleased as *Punch*, but I was a smidgen sad at the prospects of him giving up his bottle.

Still hungry from our day's activities, we settled down to share a big piece of jiffy cake I'd packed.  We ate everything but a few crumbs, which I tossed over the water.  The speckled trout, evicted earlier by our disturbance, returned to nibble our leftovers.  A combination of peacefulness and laziness left me drowsy, and I dropped off to sleep, my head resting against Toby's back.

A short time later he stirred, and I awoke with a start.  A breeze had come up which had cooled things off considerably.  Toby knew something was wrong.  He smelled it.  His shiny, black nose twitched as if somebody was tickling it with a feather.  The smell was familiar.  It was wood smoke.  "FIRE!" I shouted at him.

In a split second I crossed the brook and in the next, scampered up the opposite bank to see what I could see.  A gray, funnel-shaped splotch of smoke puffed upward somewhere over our farm, either from the barn or the sawmill.  I couldn't tell which.

Toby made no move to follow nor did I coax him.  He was safe there by the water, and he knew it.

There was no time to dawdle.  I had to make tracks for home to help.  Nightmarish thoughts gushed to mind as I climbed the side hill and raced through the pasture lot.  The cows were out of harm's way, at least.  They lay under the apple tree chewing their cuds, their cowbells tinkling softly.  Although I tried to stay calm, my legs turned to cordwood sticks, and my jaw jiggled beyond control.

I saw at once that the house was spared.  Thank God for that.  And the barn, so far.  But Dad's sawmill was an inferno, with flames shooting a hundred feet into the air.  It was being fed by the stacks of dry, seasoned wood that Dad had ready for sale, which burned like tinder.

When I finally reached the sickening sight, Mom and Dad were wetting down the side of the barn nearest it in an attempt to keep the fire from spreading to the hay.  He saw me and yelled, "Stop the first car that comes along.  Tell whoever it is to get to a telephone and call the closest fire department.  Then get old Harry out of the barn."

Down the driveway I flew and waited what seemed like an eternity before I saw a car coming over the flat. I stood in the middle of the road, waving my arms frantically. It was an ordinary black car, but I recognized it at once as our mailman, Murf's, by the small American flag attached to the hood ornament.

"Murf," I begged, "please get to the nearest telephone and call the Glencove Fire Department for us. Dad's mill is on fire, and the barn may be next. He could hear the panic in my voice, see the tears in my eyes and the flames leaping high in the sky.

He gestured with a nod and threw the car into first gear, careening around the gas pump to backtrack. His tires squealed, scattering gravel and dirt like bird shot. He flew up the road, blowing his horn to alert our relatives who owned the neighboring farms along the way.

Several, who had already seen the pillar of smoke, came running through the fields with their buckets and brooms to help. My uncle Bill helped me blindfold old Harry. He neighed and pranced and reared, but we managed to get a bridle on him eventually and led him to safety in the cow pasture. Then we joined the bucket brigade. The barn well was already pumped dry, and there was no telling how much longer the house well would last.

Those closest to the barn ran for cover when the mill's tin roof collapsed, sending sparks and cinders everywhere. The intense heat from the mill blistered the paint on the exposed side of the barn, and the dry grass beside the lean-to caught fire. Regardless of the intense heat, the men acted quickly to beat it out with their brooms and empty feed bags.

"The house well's dry too," Dad hollered, starting to salvage what he could from the barn. As we worked feverishly, lugging out hundred-pound sacks of cow feed, chicken feed, the grindstone, pitch forks and whatever else we could carry, I saw that Dad's hands were burned and bleeding from pulling on the well rope. Before we could go back for the plow and Harry's saddle, the fire truck and volunteer firemen arrived.

They stretched a hose to the brook in time to save the barn, but the lean-to crashed into Toby's bed, igniting it like a matchbox.

After the firemen got everything wet down well, they stayed a few hours longer to keep watch with Dad in case it broke out again.

They warned that the sawdust would probably smolder for days, and they'd be back to douse it one more time.

Somebody brought my towel up from the brook, but nobody mentioned seeing a tame deer.   It began to get dark and still there was no sign of Toby.   I left a bowl of milk by the back door and one in the barn, making Dad promise to leave the door open.

Our House

## 4

## **Close Call**

I woke up with a hollow, empty feeling in the pit of my stomach, fearing that Toby was gone forever. My room was unusually dark, morguelike. Then I noticed that the shades were all pulled.

"Holy Hannah. I wonder what time it is," I exclaimed, squinting at the Big Ben on my dresser. Unable to tell in the dimness, I tugged on the shade nearest me and accidentally let it fly. It flapped around the roller until the spring was spent.

"Letitia," Mom scolded, her voice ascending from somewhere below, "save the pieces."

"I'm sorry, Mom.   It was an accident," I said apologetically, pressing my nose against the screen.   "I'll get a fork right away and rewind it."

"Never mind that now.   Did you see who was here?"

I shoved the screen to one side and poked my head out of the window.   Mom sat on the cement bench feeding Toby his bottle.   I was noted for being able to cry at the drop of a hat, and this time was no exception.   At this moment I felt relief, happiness, love and gratitude all rolled into one.   By somersaulting over my bed and sliding down the bannister, I had Toby in my arms before you could say "Jack Robinson".

As I twirled him around, I caught sight of Dad staring into the mess of charred rubble that yesterday was his sawmill.   Here and there smoke escaped, like steam from a pie cooling.   He hunched his shoulders, turned and headed our way, stopping for a minute to examine the singed leaves of his prize maple.   The three of us walked up to meet him.

"It's a cryin' shame," said Mom, trying to make light of the setback for Dad's sake, but you can't cry over spilt milk." (Boy, I wish she'd said that yesterday, I thought.)

"We should be counting our blessings," said Dad, displaying his typical rosy attitude. "It could have been much worse. Those firemen saved the barn and our house. That's what was most important. The mill can be rebuilt, right, Mother?" He put his arm around her shoulders, and together we walked back down the driveway to get cleaned up for supper.

**** 

Yesterday's fire had been the scariest experience of *my* life, and talking about it gave me the jitters. "Thanks for doing my milking and letting me sleep in, Dad," I said, changing the subject.

"Who said *I* did your milking, Tish? Your *Mom's* the one to thank."

"Why, Mom, you never let on that you knew how to milk." (She was a city girl before she married Dad.)

"I learned to milk when you were knee high to a grasshopper. It's like riding a bicycle; once you learn, you never forget."

I saw Dad give her a wink.

"My hands were so raw that my sidekick had to stand in for

me."   In a rare show of public affection, he bent over to plant a kiss on the topknot of auburn curls, forgetting about the new permanent wave.   He backed away fanning the air.   "The smell alone's enough to turn up the ends of my stache," he kidded.

"Cut it out, Wes.   It can't be that bad."

"No, it's worse," he fooled, jumping out of the way of a lashing like a batter avoiding a tight pitch.

"Truce," I said with authority, joining in on the fun.

"Tish," Dad said, changing the subject.   "How soon can you get ready?"

"Why?   Where are we going?"

"First off, I want to look at the '36 Ford Uncle Wally has for sale.   I'm out of business until I pick up a new chassis for my saw. Our other errand will take us to the train depot."

"What for?" I asked innocently.

"We're never going anywhere unless we stop this clattery banging and get on our horses," Mom interrupted.

"On second thought I think I'd better stay home with Toby,"

"Why not take him with us?   We'll throw some hay in the

back of the truck for the two of you, and if it makes you feel any better, we'll put a dog strap collar on him."   "I'll fix him a bottle in case he gets thirsty and cut off a piece of clothesline for a leash," Mom offered.

"Do we dare?" I asked.   "What if we meet up with Sly?"

"Where we're going," Dad said, "that's mighty unlikely. We'll only be gone a couple of hours.   What do you say?"

I thought for a minute.   There was something more here than met the eye, because they knew how excited I was about going to Uncle Wally's house.   Ugh!   Oh, I liked Uncle Wally well enough, but his dilly of a housekeeper, Minerva, made me nervous. Why, she kept such a clean house that it made a klutzy kid like me afraid to sit down for fear of denting a pillow.   There were signs everywhere.   Beginning at the front door, #1 read, WIPE YOUR FEET, followed by #2, LEAVE YOUR SHOES HERE.   Next came, DON'T TOUCH THE WALLS.   No, Dad had something up his sleeve, and I'd better not put a fly in the ointment.

"Well, young lady?" Dad asked, seemingly impatient. "Make up your mind.   We haven't got all day."

"I'm game," I said.

\*\*\*\*

Toby lay in the hay with his hooves curled under him like a contented kitten. I wound the clothesline round and round my one hand while I ate my belated breakfast with the other, and before I knew it, we were there.

The houses on Shade Tree Lane were all similar, with brick steps and front sun porches. What made them different were the yards and the way they were kept. Rhododendron smothered one house, and wisteria vines choked another. The victory gardens (growing vegetables was part of the war effort) were slowly being transplanted back into grass and flowers. Spiny roses and gawky hollyhocks replaced the pole beans and corn stalks. Neighbors in rockers, reading *The Morning News* on their porches, peered over their eye glasses to see where the big rack truck stopped.

Dad circled the cul-de-sac and pulled to the curb before the spic-and-span house in the middle of the block. A new '46 Chevy, shiny and black, was parked in the driveway. Dad got out and went to the side door, but before he could touch the doorbell, the door opened and Uncle Wally emerged in his stocking feet. He wasn't a genuine uncle, but what Dad called woodpile relation.

"Wes," he greeted, placing his fragile hand in Dad's vise-like grip, "what brings you folks to town?"

"My mill burned down yesterday, Wallace. Went up like a paper torch."

"I'm sorry to hear that, Wes. What can I do for you?"

After Dad told him about needing a new chassis, Uncle Wally reached inside the door for his shoes. "Vi, go visit with Minerva," he called as he and Dad disappeared into the garage out back

Mom got out of the cab, wiped her feet on the doormat (note #1) and left her shoes in the vestibule (note #2).

The last time I visited here with Dad, I discovered how to wear out my welcome in a hurry, unintentional, of course. Minerva casually asked me how things were going at school. Before I could finish telling her about the lice epidemic and how the school nurse checked our heads every morning for nits, she ushered me right outside. My assurances that I didn't have any went in one ear and out the other.

The later it got the warmer it became sitting in that pile of hay. That's why I never liked going places with grownups. All you did was hurry up and wait. Pretty soon I got impatient and decided to take Toby for a walk up the street. I jumped down and then lifted him to the ground, making sure his clothesline leash was wound tightly around my hand. We walked to the turnaround and back, not realizing what a spectacle we made. People of all ages were drawn to us like mice to cheese.

"You mean it? He just stays around and doesn't run off?" asked a young boy, dumbfounded.

"Cross my heart and hope to die," I answered, going through the motions. "I know what. Who would like to feed Toby his bottle?"

"Me. Me. Me. Me," they all chorused.

"My goodness, you sound like an a cappella choirmaster with a pitch pipe.

They all laughed. "What's your name?" I asked the dumbfounded little boy wearing the suspenders.

"Newton," he answered.

"Here, Newt.   Hold the rope until I get his bottle out of the cab."

"Gee, thanks," he stammered, glowing.

****

The whole terrible thing was my fault.   I should have read Toby's signal, but I was too busy showing him off.   His nose was twitching just like yesterday.   He sensed something, but I didn't pay particular notice.   Wisely aware of immediate danger, he slipped out of his collar with no trouble whatsoever and bounded over the blue hydrangeas before we heard the first bark.

"Toby," I cried, dropping the bottle with a crash on the sidewalk.   Over hedges, under the hammock and around clothes poles I darted, trying not to lose sight of him.

Dad heard the dogs and soon overtook me.   "There's a corn field up ahead," he shouted, passing me by and narrowly dodging a low-hanging branch.   "If they're going to catch him, it'll be there in the open."

I reached the field in time to see the pack of yelping dogs, teeth bared, closing in on Toby. I cried out loud, and tears blinded me as I tried to leap over the foot-high corn. Then from out of nowhere, shots were fired. The dogs banked to the right in tight formation, fleeing to the underbrush at the edge of the field.

Seeing that they had given up the chase, I fell between the furrows sobbing with relief, knowing full well that with Dad's extraordinary speed, he'd catch my deer. I mustered the strength to stand and saw two men converging with shotguns broken. Beside them was Dad with Toby in his arms. Regaining the power in my legs, I ran to them and took my trembling baby fawn from Dad and held him tight, trying to console him.

"I can't thank you enough for saving Toby," I said to the two farmers, still panting.

"Tish," said Dad, "this is Mr. Abbott and his son, Bill. They own this farm. Early this morning that pack of dogs slaughtered a hundred pullets of theirs and left them strewn over more than an acre of ground."

"Holy cow!" I said in disbelief.

"As soon as we heard all the barking, we knew they were after something else, so that's why we fired up in the air, knowing the shots would send them fleeing for cover."   "That fawn seems as tame as a kitten.   Are you going to raise him?" young Bill asked as he reached down to pet Toby.

"I hope to," I replied, whisking the remaining tears from my cheeks.

"I'd be happy to replant any corn we've trampled," Dad said, surveying the field.

"Forget it.   I'm just glad we could help."

****

A cheering crowd greeted us when we got back to Uncle Wally's house.   Although Mom admitted to having a few anxious moments, she said she felt certain that her Wes would return with the deer like he always did a runaway calf or rebellious cow craving wild onions.   Eating them would spoil their milk for days.

Mom had already cleaned up the glass, washed off the sidewalk and counted out the cash for the '36 Ford.

I looked for Newton and found him sitting alone on the front stoop, his eyes red and swollen.

"It wasn't your fault, Newt," I said, letting him stroke Toby's back.  "It was stupid of me to let him out of the truck in the first place.  Come on, smile.  All's well that ends well, they say.  I know!  Why don't you ask Uncle Wally to bring you up to our house sometime?  We don't live in Timbuktu, you know."

"Do you think he would?" he asked, brightening considerably.

"I'll put a bug in his ear."

He was so pleased I thought he'd burst his buttons as he went whistling down the street, his thumbs bowing out his suspenders.

Toby and I retreated to the safety of the truck where we stayed put for the remainder of the trip.  With all the commotion of the past hour, I'd forgotten about the mysterious stop at the depot and was jarred when we turned in that direction.  I was so thirsty I was spitting cotton, and I knew Toby must be, too.

Dad backed up to the loading platform.  He and Mom got out of the truck and went into the station.  I still had no idea why we were here or what we were here for, and, frankly, I was too tired to care.   Although I was even more impatient than I was at Uncle Wally's house, we sat tight and waited.   Pretty soon the double doors opened and Mom and Dad emerged, followed by a man, who made Dad look small, carrying a large, rectangular-shaped box single-handedly.

I stood up, suddenly curious, spelling the letters aloud: "GIRL'S BICYCLE.   GIRL'S BICYCLE!" I screeched, jumping from down in the dumps to up in the clouds in a snap.

"Surprise!" Mom and Dad chimed in unison.

"My first bicycle.   A twenty-eight incher.   And BLUE, my favorite color," I sputtered, clapping my hands and jumping up and down.

Dad released the tailgate, and the station agent walked effortlessly into the body of the truck with Dad following.   He held me down long enough to plant a kiss on each of my cheeks. "Happy Birthday, Tish," Mom added, throwing me my kiss. Toby's clothesline wrapped around my hand and knowing what my Mom was thinking prevented me from turning a cartwheel right then and there.   *Letitia, there's a time and a place for everything.*   I agreed that this definitely was not the place but it certainly was the time.

"Thank you. Thank you. Thank you." The words gushed out like air from a pricked balloon. "Now I'll be able to keep pace with you, sea biscuit," I said to Toby, cupping his precious face in my hands. "We'll have a ball this summer."

The man, satisfied that he'd positioned the box to ride well, did a double take when he saw Toby. "Well I'll be a monkey's uncle, if it ain't a baby fawn," he exclaimed, shaking his head.

"I'm raising him," I said proudly.

"Well, I declare. My son, Hank, should see this. He's a reporter for the *Town Ledger*," he said, cowering over us like the giant from "Jack and the Beanstalk", his eyebrows arching into two bushy parentheses. It was a blessing that I was good at holding my breath, because the odor of garlic was so strong it made my eyes water, but as Mim always said, "Halitosis is better than no breath at all".

It wasn't easy keeping a straight face. Thank heavens Dad came to the rescue before I turned blue.

"Going by the Regulator clock inside, Tish, it's after noontime, so we've got to get rolling," Dad said.

"My son might want to do a story on your daughter and her deer," the man said, straightening up and addressing Dad. "Would it be all right?"

Dad shrugged his shoulders. "Can't see where it would hurt. Ask Tish. It's her pet."

"Nothing definite, you understand," the man cautioned, pivoting to face Tish. He raised one parenthesis and pulled on his lower lip, waiting for her answer.

"Why not," I replied in a rather absent tone, thinking I'd never see hide nor hair of either him or his son again.

"How long will it take me to learn to ride?" I asked Dad, climbing halfway up the rack and hanging precariously over the edge.

"Probably not as long as it will take me to assemble that contraption," Dad chuckled, starting up the motor.

****

As usual, Dad was right. It took exactly three unsuccessful

attempts before I got the hang of keeping my balance. Toby was a scream. For some reason the bicycle tires fascinated him, and he butt at them continuously as we sped along dodging holes and zigzagging around bumps and stones. Sheer physical exhaustion finally forced us to call it a day. If only I could, I would have put a chock behind the sun that afternoon to prevent it from setting.

Before dessert I fell asleep with my head on the kitchen table. "I'm not asleep," I murmured drowsily as Dad carried me upstairs. "I was just resting my eyes." But my bed felt oh so good. I savored the sweet, fresh-air smell of the sheets, sheets cooled by a gentle evening breeze, that fanned and lulled me back to sleep.

*Dad and Toby*

# 5

## What's Good For The Gander Is Good For The Goose

Because I went to bed with the chickens, my night's sleep was over before 5:00 a.m. Not wanting to disturb the rest of the household, I slipped quietly downstairs to curl up in the white wicker chair on the porch to watch the sun rise and to reread the two letters I'd gotten in yesterday's mail. Dawn was as yet only a smear of color on the horizon, like unbeaten egg whites, soft and shimmery, but by the time I finished deciphering Mim's note (the majority of it written in Pig Latin on napkins from the clubhouse), the sun had risen and lay, sunny-side up, on a mountain of dark toast.

Ancay (Can) omecay (come) otay (to) ouryay (your) irthdaybay (birthday) artypay (party). Illway (will) taysay (stay) hetay (the) eekway (week).

"What a lulu," I chuckled, putting it aside. Mim was always good for a laugh. David's letter was written on a leftover sheet of lined school paper, but who cared. He'd written. That was the important thing. "I'll come to your birthday party if you'll promise to go to the moonlight swim with me," it read.

"How lucky can I get?" I said to myself, closing my eyes dreamily and pressing the letter to my chest.

A scratchy sound interrupted my thoughts, and I looked up to see Toby peering through the screen door. "Good morning, precious," I said, rising with difficulty to let him in. "How's my doll baby today? I think I overdid it yesterday, because I'm as stiff as a board myself." I kissed the bridge of his nose and stroked his ears. "Hungry?" I asked. "I'm starving. Let's get some cereal and milk." Toby followed me into the kitchen.

"You know, young man, you rate. Listen to this." I took

David's letter out of my pajama pocket and read: "I've talked so much about Toby that my mother and father have to see him for themselves, so we'll be stopping by on Sunday afternoon."

"David's coming here *today*, thanks to you," I exploded in a giggly whisper. I talked to Toby as though he were a human. Although he could now drink from a bowl, I babied him this morning and gave him one more bottle as a thank you.

Afterwards, I laid out our plans for the day: "We'll finish our chores lickety-split. Next, we'll mow the grass and hoe the flower beds so the yard looks presentable. Then we'll go down to the swimming hole, and I'll wash my hair and bathe. "Don't let me forget a cake of soap, baby shampoo and a piece of lemon. Mim says that if you squeeze lemon juice on your hair and then sit in the sun, your hair'll get shades lighter. We'd better get the lemon now, because I have a feeling that Mom wouldn't approve of that. What's that expression Gram always uses? Oh, yeah. "What you don't know won't hurt you."

The only thing that worried me was that Mom had a knack of knowing everything. Nobody could pull the wool over her eyes.

Oh well, if she did suspect, I'd just have to tell the truth.  I wouldn't dare fib, since Mom believed that a liar was worse than a thief.

Toby never seemed to tire of my idle chatter.  He was more than a pet.  He was my friend.

**\*\*\*\***

Even with company coming, I couldn't wriggle out of going to church.  Fr. Barry arrived like clockwork, and I hopped into the station wagon to be driven to the mission.  Martha and I played cat's cradle all the way there to make the time pass quickly.  If I ever prayed for a short sermon, it was today, but no such luck. David was already there when Fr. Barry dropped me off at the end of the driveway.

"Thank you.  Bye everybody," I said slamming the door. "How long have you been here?" I hollered to David as he and Toby ran down to meet me.

"About fifteen minutes is all," he answered.

"So, what do you think of my pride and joy?" I asked, glowing.  I put my hat on Toby and fastened the elastic under his chin.

"I'm jealous."

"You mean *you* want to wear my hat?" I joked.

"I mean it explains your one-track mind, silly." He grabbed my hand and ushered me toward the foursome who were enjoying tall glasses of, oh my goodness, *lemonade*. I blushed from a teeny bit of guilt, hoping my hair's added sheen wasn't noticeable.

After everyone exchanged niceties and laughed over Toby's nonchalance, Mr. Dwyer asked, "Wasn't that a priest who brought you home, Tish?"

"Yes, Mr. Dwyer, that was Fr. Barry."

"I didn't know there was a Catholic church on this side of town."

"He runs St. Paul's mission, but his big church is in Twin Falls."

"But I thought that mission was a negro church," he continued.

"No. It's just a regular Episcopal mission. Anybody may go there."

"You folks must know Mrs. Kelly," Dad said, breaking the

awkward silence.

"Certainly," Mrs. Dwyer replied. "She's the president of our association this year."

"Wonderful person," added Mom. "She stopped by this morning to pick up some eggs and buttermilk. By the way, Tish, before I forget, she wants you to work tomorrow."

"What kind of work do you do for her?" asked Mrs. Dwyer.

"I clean the house and do any ironing that needs to be done."

"Mr. Dwyer bit his lip and checked his watch. What time is your Jr. lifesaving lesson, three o'clock, David? We'd better be going."

"Golly, Dad. We just got here," he argued, pleading with his eyes.

Judging from the look he got, he's lucky he didn't get backhanded. "Write!" he formed the word but made no sound as he got into the back seat.

"I will," I promised silently, waving.

****

After working all the next day in the sweltering heat, I was in no mood for Sly, but there he was, leaning out of his truck window

shaking his finger at Dad when my cousin dropped me off.  By the

tone of his voice, I knew something had happened, and by the same

token, I could tell that Dad was trying his darndest to appease him.

"Last warning, Wes," I heard him say as he backed out and sped

away.

"What's he so riled up about now?" I asked.

"When he drove in today, he found Toby in the chicken run."

"I don't believe it!" I exclaimed.  "How'd he get in there

anyhow?"

"Our well has recovered some but not enough to do a week's

washing.  You know that.  Mrs. Crowley offered to let your

mother do our laundry at her house.  As you also know, wet wash

is mighty heavy, so Mrs. Crowley helped her bring it back and hang

it up; that is, she did the hanging while your mother made them some

lunch."

"Was she afraid of him?  Toby wouldn't hurt a fly."

"It seems that your little angel pestered the livin' daylights

out of her.  He pulled the clothes off the line as fast as she pinned them on."

"Toby did that?" I laughed, clamping my hand over my mouth.

"Yes, that scalawag. He tormented her so that she locked him up. You can't blame her. She didn't know."

Toby came from behind the barn and stood licking the salt off my arm. "You rascal, you. Have you been Peck's bad boy today?"

"I think Sly's serious, Tish," said Dad. "He's issued an ultimatum. If he catches him confined one more time, he'll take him away and put him in a game preserve.

"You mean *pen him up?*"

Dad shook his head.

*Heating the curling iron*

## 6

## Double Trouble

Toby and I had more leeway now that I had a bicycle, and we spent every spare minute together, steering clear of Sly. Every day was a new and exciting adventure. We followed overgrown wood roads through the mountains for miles, stopping to track down a noisy, red-tailed woodpecker or to rest under a rambling oak to watch a pair of zany gray squirrels perform daring acrobatic feats. I'd clown around, making believe it was a command performance just for us. "Encore. Encore," I cheered, which immediately brought down the curtain. After a brief intermission, however, the stage-struck twosome overcame their stage fright and played to their heart's content, ignoring the harmless audience.

The damp ground was cool and mossy, a welcome relief after almost melting picking icky potato bugs. Overhead an awning of elm, oak and maple leaves shaded us from the blistering sun. "This is heaven," I said to Toby, who was milling around taste testing all sorts of vegetation. Tender sprigs of fern blanketed the banks on either side of the brook, and he liked them almost as much as the lacy carrot tops he'd sampled in the garden earlier. "Dad will tan both our hides if he catches you in that carrot patch, you little scamp. Come on. Let's go see how high the falls are."

I parked my bike, leaning it securely against the kickstand, and scrambled down the slope. Mountain laurel blossoms, shed only recently, littered the path. Toby had stopped to browse on the delicate young shoots, finding them very satisfying. I backtracked to make sure he wasn't feeding on a staggerbush, one of the few poisonous plants, but nothing around fit Dad's description of it, so I left him alone and continued on ahead.

The fast-moving water skittered over stones and around fallen limbs. It reminded me of Minerva's spanking clean windows--so spotlessly clear you couldn't tell whether they were open or shut. I flopped to the ground guzzling my fill before scooping up handfuls to splash on my face. Refreshed, I gave Toby a whistle and sauntered on toward the falls.

The first drop was nothing spectacular, but from the base of the second cascade, it looked like the mouth of a pitcher pouring frothy milk twenty feet into a giant cereal bowl below. "Wow! This is really groovy!" *Wow! This is really groovy!* my voice echoed. I've got to remember to bring Mim here, I thought. She'll get a charge out of this. Of course, I couldn't resist doing "Little Sir Echo". By the time I sang the second line, the first one was already reverberating. It was like singing a round all by myself. I dawdled away about fifteen minutes in this idle amusement before Toby finally joined me.

"Hi, sugarfoot," I greeted, raising my voice above the water's boil. "Are you having fun? You must be thirsty. How about a drink?" I cupped my hands and dished up some water for him, but he moved away from the torrent to where the ripples flattened out and drank by himself until his sides bulged.

"You little piggy," I teased. "I bet you're ready for a rest."

He wandered off among the hemlocks nearby while I dangled my feet in the foaming eddy, the spray showering me like a spring rain. There was a magical fascination in the sound and motion of the rushing water, and it held me spellbound, like the ocean surf at Pt. Pleasant had done.

Sometime later I shivered, and the spell was broken. My feet felt like two icicles but looked more like two purple plums. Slanted rays of sunlight filtered through the trees, and I didn't need a watch to tell me that it was time to head home. I wound myself up like a pretzel, trying to dry my feet on the bottom of my shirt.

"Come on Toby. Time to go." Glancing in his direction, I was awed by a strange phenomenon. I'd seen it before but never up close. Dad said the sun was drawing water. It was a weird sight, yet beautiful. It created the effect of slanted slats of dark and light bars starting in heaven and zeroing in on a place beneath, like the newfangled thing in the dentist's office he called a Venetian blind (only up and down, not crossways).

Wouldn't it be nifty if this happened when I brought Mim

here, I thought, because as she always says, seeing's believing.

A slight stirring of the leaves, a shift in the angle of the setting sun and in the snap of a finger, Toby was no longer in the limelight. A second shiver brought me back to reality, and I reached down to pick up my socks from the flat rock where I'd left them.

A wriggly motion drew my attention and I froze. The wriggly motion was the tail of a copperhead, and the other end, the end that scared me more, was poised over the Lincoln head penny in one of my loafers. The snake was a young one, skinny, probably not more than eighteen inches all stretched out, but young or not, it was just as deadly.

"Toby," I whispered, trying desperately to keep my head and hand steady. My mouth puckered into a whistle, but no sound came. Stealthily, Toby moved nearer and nearer. Wham! He hit the snake hard with his sharp hooves, stunning it, scoring right behind the head. He whacked and whacked until I called him off. I had become suddenly brave after Toby's first blow and went to get a rock. I closed my eyes tight and let go. Boom! I peeked.

"Egad," I said to him, "he's dead as a doornail."

I picked my steps carefully up the side of the ravine, keeping Toby close beside me. If we met up with a small copperhead, sure as shootin' the big, fat thick ones weren't far away.

It wasn't until we were safely out of the woods that I began to shake. Maybe it was the looks of that thing draped over a stick across the wire basket on the front of my bike that gave me the willies. "I'm going to pickle him like pig's feet," I told him, trying to laugh. "Then we'll show it to Sly."

****

Toby and I stuck around the farm the next week, not that we were chicken or anything. The furthest we ventured was down to the swimming hole to take a dip to cool off. Mom's philosophy was "idle hands, idle mind," so after the creepy business of preserving Toby's snake was behind me, to keep everything copacetic, I started to double up on my practicing. There was a method in my madness, of course. This way, when Mim came for her week's visit the following Saturday, I wouldn't bore her with Hanons, because her speed was chopsticks.

David answered my letter with a postcard from baseball camp saying that he was coming to my birthday party but could only stay from six to eight o'clock. Two measly hours, I thought. That irked the dickens out of me. I got out my trusty list and tried to figure out how we'd fit everything into that length of time:

Picnic supper - one hour

Toby - a quarter of an hour

Presents - a quarter of an hour

Games - one-half hour

Mim's suggestion was beginning to sound more and more sensible. Forget hide-and seek and get right to the kissing games. She's a doozie, I thought. That must be how an extrovert thinks. An introvert like she says I am would stick to the game plan. Mom said we're a good example of how opposites attract.

Why is it that when you're looking forward to something special, time seems to stand still? And wouldn't you know it? It had to rain all week in the bargain. I worked one day at my housekeeping job and earned another five dollars. That night, while Mom and Dad listened to Lowell Thomas on the radio, I stacked and counted and counted and stacked my money.  Also on the kitchen table was the "wish book", opened to the bathing suit page.

"You're going to wear them out just looking at them," Dad teased when the news was over.  "What's the matter?  Are those sawbucks burning a hole in your pocket?"

"You can't have your cake and eat it too, Mom mimicked, turning up the wick on the kerosene lamp and pushing it gently across the porcelain-topped table to my side.  This business of playing shuffleboard with the lamp always reminded me of our rip-roaring Sunday night pinochle games when no one wanted this hot nuisance in his corner, and, as a result, they jostled it around from one to another.  "I swear, Tish, you're going to have that book memorized."

"I know I need a new suit for the moonlight swim.  My old one is all stretched out.  But this is the first time I've bought anything with my very own hard-earned money, and, for some reason, it's different.  It ain't the same as spending money I've gotten for birthdays or Christmases.  Is that what you mean when you say 'easy come, easy go?'"

"When you sweat to make it," Dad said, you think twice before you spend it."

I returned to the book to rethink it. "Sold!" I said decisively, filling out the order form. "The flowered suit with the triangular-shaped cutout just above the waistline." It was a little daring, and I was surprised Mom didn't object. Maybe it was because on Saturday, I was going to be a teenager. It had been a full day, and I was bushed, so I climbed the wooden hill and went to bed.

****

Because my friends, the conglomeration of birds housed in the maple outside my bedroom window, didn't wake me with their early-morning chitchat, I knew before opening my eyes that we were in for another dreary, drizzly day. Farmers welcomed a spell of rainy weather now and then. Crops sprouted, wells filled, and they got a chance to sit back and rest on their laurels, catching up on their reading and repairing.

That's exactly what I felt like doing, curling up with Toby

and reading a good book. I didn't have much choice. It was either "Pollyanna" or the encyclopedia. Our fifth-grade teacher had set up our first library in the basement of our school, but we weren't allowed to take books home over the summer. Of course, I chose to read "Pollyanna" for the umpteenth time and retrieved it from the shelf over the roll top desk. I thought of smuggling Toby up to my room, but with my luck, old Sly would show up and smell a rat, or, more likely, Mom would have a conniption fit. Instead, I settled for Toby's abode, a cozy corner of the barn alongside the feed bins, with hay for bedding and a couple of sacks of chicken mash for pillows. I left the barn door wide open so Toby wasn't confined.

He listened patiently, his sensitive ears perked up one minute, prone the next, reacting to the humdrum or the excited pitch of my voice. We had just gotten to the part where Mrs. Snow and the undertaker had decided that her casket should have satin lining and gold handles and Pollyanna was scolding her for always thinking about dying instead of living when Henrietta sidled up against my leg purring, with a dead mouse in her mouth.

Eeek!" I shrieked, leaping up on the feed bins behind me.

"Skidoo!"

Toby only stretched and yawned, blinking at the square of sun squeezing through the cobwebby window.

"The sun," I yelled, jumping down and forgetting about being scared. I rushed outside and scanned the sky for the first sign of a rainbow. The rain felt cold but delicious, unlike the hot shower I loved so at Mim's house. Only here, I pictured a giant watering can sprinkling the earth with a fine, steady spray.

"Mom! Dad!" I shouted giddily. "Look!"

Mom signaled from the porch with her dish towel, and they stood, arm in arm, taking a minute out to enjoy the all-too-brief magic show with me.

"Ain't it gorgeous, Toby?" I exclaimed, biting my tongue. I hadn't meant to be a copycat, but I knew I sounded for all the world like Pollyanna herself.

The storm clouds scudded over us heading northeast, tumbling over one another in their haste, causing mountainous pileups here and contrasting blotches of blue there. The sky looked like the three-ring circus I'd seen once, with everything happening at the same time.

Right then and there, muddy or not, I did a cartwheel, because I was tickled pink that I was going to have a nice day for my birthday party after all.

****

And a nice day it was, clear and balmy, with no hu-mi-di-ty, as Arthur Godfrey always said. All the preparations went along smoothly. The cake didn't fall, the boiled eggs peeled without sticking, and my hair behaved. I made Toby a black and white bow tie, which he wore without any fuss whatsoever.

Mim saw to it that David and Artie didn't renege. She brought them with her.

"Hi, party girl," David greeted, handing me a small, square, gift-wrapped box. "I hope you like it."

"Thank you," I said, taking it from him. "I'm sure I will." As our fingers touched we both got a slight shock and laughed. David had an attraction that was hard to explain, but I think it was the way he smelled, clean and fresh, like a basket of Mom's folded laundry.

"Happy birthday, pal," said Mim, hugging me.

"Where's your suitcase?" I asked anxiously.

"Don't worry.  I didn't forget a thing."

"You can say that again," Mrs. Greene chuckled.  "You'd think she was staying for the summer."

"Could she?" I begged hopefully.

"No, dear.  Pity your poor mother."

Artie said hello in his usual shy manner and thrust a bulky package into my arms.

"Thanks, Artie.  I'm glad you could come."

"Give me the keys, Mrs. Greene, and we'll get Mim's stuff out of the trunk," said David.

"Thanks, boys."

Toby, who so far was the center of attention, was entertaining the rest of the group by acting silly and kicking up his heels when he was petted, kissed or hugged.

"Holy crow!" exclaimed Artie returning from delivering Mim's baggage, "a deer wearing a bow tie.  I never would have believed it unless I saw it with my own two eyes."

"Isn't he a sweetheart?"

"Tish," Mim said, "let me hold those presents. You've got to open mine right this minute."

"Mom's got supper on the table, and I thought we'd save this until later."

"Please, Tish,"

"Okay, if you insist."

"Be careful. Don't drop it."

I tore off the paper and shouted, "A Brownie® camera!"

"It's loaded and ready to go. Get a shot of Toby this instant, before he decides to undress. It'll be a classic." Mim's green eyes glittered with excitement.

I was so choked up that David had to take the picture. I gave Mim a bear hug and she understood.

"You can have fun taking pictures of him as he grows up. Come on. No tears. You'll look ugly," she added, making me laugh.

"I can see you two are going to have a ball. Bye, love," said Mrs. Greene. "We'll pick you up next Sunday."

"Bye, Mom," she said, going to the car to kiss her mother. "Thanks for bringing me."

"Yeah, thanks for the ride," Artie and David said in unison.

"Anytime, boys," she replied and drove away.

Mom rang the dinner bell, and everybody let out a war whoop and raced to dig in.

"If Tish's grandmother were here, do you know what she'd say?" Mim asked importantly.

Everyone stopped eating and chorused: "Eat when you're hungry; drink when you're dry. If you never get sick, you'll live 'til you die."

"Oh, you spoilsports," said Mim, a little downcast. "You've all heard it before."

"Eat," said Mom, setting down another platter of baked ham. Pass the potato salad and noodle salad around, Tish. Laurie didn't get any yet. I've got another dish of baked beans when that one's gone."

"I think we just need another bottle of root beer, Mom," I said seeing how fast the first one was disappearing.

I was too keyed up to eat. It took Mim to get the party moving again (away from the table) by suggesting that she take a picture of David and me posing under the rose arbor.

"How tender," the girls all cooed. David blushed a smidgen and removed his arm from around my shoulder once he heard the click.

"Now that that's over," I said, pretending that I minded too, "I think it's time to open those interesting-looking presents."

"Just sit down in a circle on the grass," said Mim, the organizer, "and I'll bring the packages."

Everyone agreed, even Toby, who flopped down next to me."

"Well now," David whispered (only loud enough for me to hear), "competition is one thing, but playing second fiddle to a deer is embarrassing."

It was my turn to blush, because if I read his remark correctly, he considered me *his girl.*

I opened Artie's first. "A blue beach towel. Now that's a handy gift," I said, standing up so everyone could see it.

"KILROY WAS HERE," Frank spurted out as it unfolded.

"That takes the cake, Artie," Mim said, giving him an affectionate shove with her shoulder.

Among the other six gifts, which were all deer related, were a book called "The Yearling" and two movie tickets to see "Bambi". I opened David's last. "An identification bracelet," I gasped. "It's so beautiful, David. Thank you." I unfastened it carefully from the taffeta-covered backing and had Mim put it on me.

"Is it engraved?" asked Sally.

"Uh huh. It says, TISH."

Before you do, don't," said Mim, raising her finger in the air to halt the tears.

"Ah, look," said Laurie. Mom had lighted the candles in the kitchen and was on her way out to the picnic table singing as she came. Soon everyone joined in. As they neared the end, I drew in a deep breath and "Whoooo". I blew out all fourteen candles?

"One for good luck," Mom said as she kissed me on the cheek.

Mim kicked my foot under the table, so I mentioned

offhandedly that if everyone was finished eating, we'd play a few games. The boys went for seconds while the girls got set up for Spin the Bottle. I pumped away at the flit can to ward away pesky mosquitoes while the others spread a quilt on the lawn.

"Who wants to be first?" Mim asked, luring the boys away from the food by waving the milk bottle. (I was relieved that Mim was handling this part of the party for me, but, of course, it was only natural, since she was the extrovert.) When no one bit, she asked, "Do we have to waste time doing One Potato, Two Potato, or will someone be brave?"

"I'll be first," said Sally, raising her hand timidly.

"Round and round and round it goes. Where it stops, nobody knows. Artie," said Doug, acting like the head monkety-monk. "Come on, Sally, kiss him. Mim won't look."

That broke the ice, and from then on everyone relaxed and had a hilarious time. Mim was flustered because she only got to kiss Artie twice, so she kiddingly turned over the breadboard to see whether the bottle would spin better on the other side. When that didn't work either, she said, "I'm tired of this game. Let's play

Snub."

"The boys volunteer to set it up *and* go first," said Doug.

"That's a switch," said Mim rather suspiciously.

They got two kitchen chairs and placed them side by side facing in opposite directions. Artie sat down first. He snubbed each girl in succession until he got to me. I was as shocked as Mim when I got kissed. Anyhow, Mim had the last laugh, because David snubbed me and kissed her. We agreed that the whole thing was premeditated and although we had a chance to get even, decided not to be copycats.

As a result, I was kissing David when his parents walked into the yard. David was embarrassed and knew from their scowls that they disapproved and that he was in for a dressing down on the way home.

David and Artie's leaving put a damper on the party, and after that, nobody was in the mood to play Post Office; instead, as in the beginning, Toby was the big attraction.

*The Barn, Dad and Harry the Horse*

# 7

# A Little White Lie

Mim and I yackety-yakked for hours, until Mom tiptoed in and told us to go to sleep. She knew us, knew we'd be up early full of vim and vigor, trying to cram two days' activities into one for the entire next week.

With two more helping hands, the chores were a breeze. Mim pitched right in. She was a real trooper, not afraid to get her hands dirty. She cleaned stables, ranked wood or churned butter with equal enthusiasm. She even tried her hand at milking old Bell.

One morning as she stood with Toby watching us do the milking, Dad asked, "Mim have you ever seen a cow laugh?" (I'd been waiting for this.)

"No, Mr. Armstrong," she replied in all seriousness, all eyes. (I wanted to warn her but knew it would spoil the fun.)

Zing! Dad let her have it with a long squirt of milk right in the kisser. Well, you never heard such squealing and carrying on in all your born days. Dad haw hawed until I thought he'd split a seam, like he always did when he played his prank on an unsuspecting greenhorn. When the hilarity subsided, he showed Mim how expert Toby had become at guzzling that long stream of warm milk from a distance of five feet or so.

Just as hilarious was the sight of the three of us on our daily excursions, Mim and I on the bike and Toby running alongside butting at the wheels. We picnicked under our favorite pine by the brook and even ventured back to the falls to show her the place where Toby saved my life. To be on the safe side, I borrowed Dad's hand-hewn walking stick, and we proceeded timidly, like a convoy through a minefield, single file. Although we reached the falls without incident, before we had a chance to yodel, Mim saw an eel and yelled, "Snake!" We broke ranks and fled helter skelter up the bank, our flight resembling an old-fashioned Laurel and Hardy two-reel comedy.

By Saturday we'd shown her most of our secret places, made homemade blueberry ice cream, using the berries we'd picked in the meadow, pulled taffy and evened our tans, so when Dad said he needed help getting in a load of dry hay before it stormed, we didn't mind in the least.

He hitched old Harry to the wagon, and we all climbed in with our pitchforks and rakes.

"Don't know if we can beat it or not," he said, studying the blackness that was spreading across the sky like spilled ink. He tapped Harry lightly with the reins to prod him along.

The field was partitioned by a half dozen windrows, and we rode to the farthest one. Dad and I loaded while Mim trampled it down. The hay stuck to our sweaty skin like poppy seeds to a roll. We worked faster and faster, gobbling up windrow after windrow. The thunder grumbled and growled, like a mad dog ready to attack. The lightning hacked away at the sky, dealing it blow after blow. The wind rose from a whisper to a roar, and Dad had to shout above it to be heard.

"Tish, get up there with Mim and help her hold the load down.   We're heading for the barn."

Obeying, I stepped on the whiffletree, and from there Mim hoisted me up.

The leaves wrestled with the wind, turning them wrong side out, a sure sign that rain was on its way, according to Mom.   Dad grabbed old Harry's halter and led him a short distance when, all of a sudden, one of the wagon wheels sank into a groundhog hole. The hay shifted and slid.

"Oh, no.   Here we go," Mim and I yelled.   Powerless to save ourselves, we became part and parcel of the avalanche.

Letting go of old Harry, Dad ran to uncover us.   We surfaced spitting, sputtering and coughing.   "Are you hurt?"

"No," we both chimed.   "Just full of hayseed!" I added.

"Can you use two extra scarecrows, Mr. Armstrong?" Mim joshed, removing the worried lines from Dad's face.

"My heart was in my throat there for a minute. But I have to admit, it was funny."

Mim and I took a good look at each other and burst out

laughing. Hayseed clung to her black, curly hair like powder to a wig. Spikes of rye grass anchored themselves to mine like briars to burlap. Once we realized that we were all in one piece, our mouths went like whippoorwills rehashing our dramatic experience. Old Harry, on the other hand, the wise one, not feeling any pressure on the bit in his mouth, ambled to the barn with the remnants of his load.

Totally lacking in manners nature didn't wait until we reached the barn before letting off her steam but drenched us thoroughly on the way. It rained pitchforks and hammer handles, but Toby lay snug as a bug in a rug, having had sense enough to go in out of the rain. Mim's teeth chattered, and I shivered like I had Saint Vitus's dance.

"You two better make a beeline for the house and change into some dry clothes," said Dad as he unhitched Harry and got him in his stall, "or you'll both have your death of cold."

Dad never got colds. He said it was because of all the bacon grease he ate, a whole bowlful every morning soaked up in a half a loaf of bread. Ugh!

"Do you think Mom'll holler if I bring Toby into the house until this is over?" I ventured.

"Maybe as far as the porch. I wouldn't push my luck. She's anxious about us, though. I see her at the kitchen window. Run along and tell her I'll be down as soon as I get some water and hay for Harry."

I wrapped Toby in a feed sack and, carrying him, made a mad dash. I noticed that he was much heavier than the last time I'd picked him up, but we made it. We told Mom what happened to us, laughing all the time, not wanting her to be more upset than we saw she already was. After drying off and getting into warm chenille housecoats, we huddled together on the porch glider, bystanders to nature's vicious attack.

We tried to be brave for Toby's sake and Mom's, but the lightning stabbed at objects closer and closer and terrified us. One strike hit a clothes pole, splintering it into kindling wood. All of a sudden we both screamed, "NO!" Mom came running! Lightening had made a direct hit on the barn pump and Dad's hand seemed to be stuck to the pump handle. Without a second's hesitation, Mom ran out into the storm and up the driveway. We watched all of this wide-eyed, with mouths open. The next minute, thank goodness, Dad was shaking off the effects of his close call and Mom was carrying the pail of water to Old Harry. We breathed a sigh of relief when we saw them standing arm in arm in the safety of the barn.

They were wise to stay put, because within minutes another bolt knifed its way through the black clouds and struck a disastrous blow on Dad's enormous maple tree. By this time, we were *under* Mom's crocheted afghan peering through the holes. We heard the c-r-a-c-k and tore off the blanket in time to see the tree that had shaded the driveway for generations split in half as though it were a toothpick. Dad couldn't have made a cleaner splice with his ax.

"Good grief," I shuddered, looking at Mim. She was speechless, which was a rarity.

Having accomplished its mission, the storm finally skirted over us, leaving senseless destruction in its wake.

****

"What a pity," said Mom, rubbing Dad's arm gently.

"It could have been worse, Evvy. It could have fallen on the barn. I wonder how your mother and the others in the valley fared?"

Mim and I followed Mom and Dad up to see the hewn giant gingerly, expecting a Japanese jujitsu artist or Merlin the magician to spook us at any minute and claim responsibility.

Someone *did* appear. It was Sly, on foot, which was odd. His hair was plastered to his head, his shirt dripping wet. His face was redder than usual, and I noticed for the first time a wide space between his two front teeth where he cradled his tongue, like a viper getting ready to strike.

"You think you got troubles, Wes," he complained, glancing disinterestedly at Dad's slaughtered maple. "I almost got killed. An oak uprooted and fell smack on the hood of my truck."

"Are you hurt?" Dad asked, looking him over.

"No, but my truck is a mess, and I need help to clear the road so I can get out of here; otherwise, I'm stranded."

"You and a lot of other people," Dad added. I'll get my truck and my saw. Tish, draw a bucket of water and give him a drink.

Toby, who had been nibbling on some juicy, wet grape leaves that covered the entire length of the chicken run fence, followed me to the well. Sly went to pet him, but Toby backed away. "Unfriendly little cuss," he said.

"Not really. It's just that his senses are keen," I explained.

"His fur's dry. Where'd you keep him during the storm?"

"He was in the barn," I replied, crossing my fingers. I figured that was a partial truth. "We left the barn door open," I added quickly, fearing a confrontation.

He slurped long draughts of water from the ladle. Dad tooted and Sly got into the truck.

"Toby weathered the storm better than you did, Sly," said Mom, rubbing a little salt in the wound. Then, turning to me, she said, "And you and I, young lady, are going to have a talk about telling that falsehood. You must *never lie!*"

"Well, Toby *was* in the barn *before* he was on the porch," I rationalized.

Mom went back into the house shaking her head.

*Toby with Dickey and Mickey*

## 8

## The Losing End Of The Stick

I didn't need to have a ton of bricks fall on my head to know that David's parents objected to me, so I wasn't surprised when I got his note the following week saying he wouldn't be able to take me to the moonlight swim, because he had to go to the seashore with his mother and father.

I moped around a few days feeling sorry for myself, turning into a real crybaby, before I decided that puppy love was for the birds. Disappointed and angry, I tore up his note and threw it into one of Mom's blazing, early-morning wood fires, hoping it would cure the nagging hurt in my chest.

It worked for John Duel that Sunday night last winter when the cards weren't running his way. He finally said," Has anyone ever seen Jack jump?" Everybody else was concentrating so hard on his own hand that no one paid much attention. Well, John turned around, lifted the lid on the stove and threw his entire hand into the roaring fire.

I dashed a quickie off to Mim to let her know I wouldn't be coming. Several days later I got her reply:

"Who wants to go to a dumb old moonlight swim anyway and get eaten alive with mosquitoes? Phooey on that idea. Instead, Mom and Dad offered to take you, me, Artie and our new neighbor, Chappy, to Paradise Park. We won't take no for an answer. We'll pick you up at 5:00 p.m. Be ready!

Love, Mim

P.S. Hubba hubba. (No, it's not pig

Latin.)   It's an expression the summer gals used

when they first set eyes on Chappy."

"What a dilly," I said to Toby, wagging my head in disbelief.

"Mim's not happy unless everybody's got a crush on somebody all

the time.   My reply read:

"I accept your invitation.   STOP.   Dutch

treat only.   STOP.   Whoopee!   STOP."

Love, Tish

****

Poor Toby.   All he heard all week was Paradise Park.

Paradise Park.   I sounded like a broken record.   By Saturday he

was probably happy when I left with Dad to deliver a load of wood

so that he could have some peace and quiet.

"You get that child back here by 3:30 so she's not late.   You

hear me, Wes?" Mom warned, tugging at his sleeve.

''I promise, Vi, that we won't let any grass grow under our

feet.   You can bet your bottom dollar on that."   Dad chewed on a

tooth pick like some men sucked on a wad of nasty chewing tobacco.

He hoisted himself up into the cab beside me whistling "Billy Boy", one of his favorite tunes.

I picked up the harmony, but because the rutty road was like a washboard and it was hard to keep our voices from quavering off key, we nodded in agreement and left "charming Billie" for another day.  Instead, we rode the rest of the way in silence, unable to hear without shouting over the noise of the motor.

"Do you think we'll get a tip today?" I asked as we stopped just ahead of a mailbox marked "Silas".  "If I make a dollar today, I'll have ten dollars to spend tonight."

"We'll see.  I've heard they're frugal but very nice. Actually, it's been rumored that they'd squeeze a penny through a knothole if they could.

"Look at that climb!" I exclaimed.  "Where's the house?"

"At the top of those 100 steps."

"Egads and little fishes."

"Well," said Dad, taking a long, deep breath, " the faster we get started the sooner we get done."

"The Silases, I noticed, when they met us at the mountaintop, were a tight-lipped, jittery little pair, directing us to the cellar where the wood was to be stacked. Never leaving the basement during

our entire laborious trek, they studied each armful as we deposited

it as instructed. At last we emptied the truck of the whole cord

(which seemed like ten). At that point the pair left us and went up

into the house.

"I wonder if you'll have trouble collecting your money," I

whispered to Dad as we sat on the top cellar step resting and catching

a breath of air.

"We'll soon see."

The Silases came out of the house and surprised the life out

of us. They had cold towels and large tumblers of lemonade, but

their grateful smiles were even more refreshing.

"We've been hard workers all our lives and respect this rare

quality in others," said Mrs. Silas with unusual dignity.

"People who take pride in their work should not go

unrewarded," said Mr. Silas, handing Dad his cash for the wood,

plus a dollar tip. He also deposited a dollar bill into my hand.

"Thanking them, we all shook hands and waved goodbye.

"See, Tish, they weren't such bad eggs after all. You've got to take people the way *you* find them and not listen to hearsay."

"They were sweet, in a funny sort of way, and very generous," I said fingering the folded bill in my pocket.

****

An amusement park, I learned that night, is no place to take every nickel you own. My money evaporated like a pipedream. Mim suggested we start on the scariest ride, the bobsled, because, in comparison, all the others would be tame. It sounded like a logical idea; anyhow, who was I to argue? Up to this point in my life, the most exciting ride I ever had was down Aunt Sarah's hill on a sled playing hitch toboggan.

As we climbed to the top of the first pinnacle, even though Chappy was a relative stranger, I asked him if he minded putting his arm around me.

"Happy to," he replied with a smile.

From the moment we tipped over the brink of the first dip, I sealed my eyes shut and dug my head into Chappy's shoulder, clinging to him for dear life.

Mim and Artie didn't look too chipper either when they got

off.   That ride was wild enough to take the starch out of all of us for a while.   Even daredevil Mim simmered down and agreed to a peaceful boat ride.

That gave me a chance to apologize to Chappy for being so forward on the bobsled.   "Think nothing of it," he said as he maneuvered the slow-moving boat around a hairpin turn.   "You want to know a secret?" he added, looking me straight in the eye. "I was scared out of my wits."

"You're very nice," I said with a smile.

"You know," he said, changing the subject, "I still can't get Toby out of my mind.   What a pet!"

"He's the berries, all right.

"Mim tells me the state's itching to take him away from you, that they want to put him in a preserve or something."

"It's crazy, Chappy.   Sly, he's the warden, seems to be obsessed with Toby.   Everything's hunky-dory if *he* were to confine him, but when the shoe's on the other foot, it's against the law.

"I have an idea," he mused.   "Why don't you make Toby

your school mascot and circulate a petition asking the state to let you keep him until *he* wants to leave."

"Do you think it would work?" I asked, jerking myself around to face him, causing the boat to hit the side of the channel.

"It's worth a try.  What've you got to lose?"

\*\*\*\*

Chappy's suggestion gave me a lot to think about over the rest of the summer; in fact, I was so preoccupied that I didn't even notice that my spindlelegs had suddenly filled out to conceal my knobby knees.

Kit noticed right away the Sunday Dad took me to visit her and Henry.  I found her down by the pond checking a portion of last year's trapline.  She was dressed, as usual, despite the sickening heat, in her mended slacks and one of Henry's work shirts.  Even though I only had on a pair of shorts and a sleeveless blouse, I was clammy with sweat and felt for all the world like a slimy, fresh-caught fish.

"Go take a dunk," said Kit, who never stood on ceremony. "Your clothes'll dry in a jiffy."

"Thanks anyway, but I can't. Mom's afraid I'll get polio swimming in a lake that's purging during Dog Days. I got my orders before I left."

"God forbid," said Kit, "let's not even talk about that dreadful disease. Come on. We'll go sit on the porch and have a cold drink of tea while you tell me all about Toby's latest antics."

Like a proud parent, I bragged on and on, especially about how he killed the snake. "Oh, by the way, I pickled the copperhead and brought him with me to show you." I ran to the car to fetch the jar and met up with Dad, Harry and his dog, Ernie, his faithful sidekick.

"What is Ernie, Harry?" I always asked the same question but never got the same answer. He was ready for me this time and came back with a beauty.

"Well," he said, stopping to stroke his angular, clean-shaven chin, "I'd say he's a pointer and a setter."

"Why's that?" I asked with tongue in cheek.

"Because," said Harry, "he sets all day and points at the stove."

"That's a real corker, Henry," I cackled. His dry sense of humor made it twice as funny.

"You missed your calling," said Dad. "You should have been a stand-up comedian.

"Who killed the copperhead?" Henry asked, tapping my mason jar with the bowl of his pipe. "Certainly not this little pip-squeak!" he added, tugging my pigtail.

"Toby's the hero," said Dad. "He saved her life."

"That a fact. Trounced on it with his hooves, I bet. Deer'll do that."

"I was petrified but not Toby. He was a brave, little soldier."

"Why, that deer must be the cat's meow!"

"He's more than that," I answered. "He's my friend."

We stepped up onto the far end of the porch where a large, wooden box, taller than I was, took up most of the space. "What's in there?" I asked inquisitively.

"A whole *slew* of poisonous snakes," said Henry.

"What in heaven's sake for?"

"It's a job. We catch them alive for the zoo in the city. Do you want to take a gander at them?"

"Of course I do. I'm not a scaredy-cat."

Dad lifted me piggyback fashion. Henry pinned down a six-foot rattler right behind its head with a two-pronged stick, causing it to vibrate its tail and rattle. This set the rest of the swarm in motion, squiggling over, under and around each other.

"Eeek!" I screamed, clamping my eyes closed and burrowing my face into Dad's back. "Put me down! Put me down!" As I slid to the porch, I came face to face with Toby's pickled copperhead that I'd been clutching in my arm. I heaved it into the yard, smashing the jar to smithereens against the fence and ran into Kit's arms.

****

On the way home I sat close to Dad with my head against his sleeve. "I feel like such a jerk. I'm sorry I acted like such a baby."

"Tish, I ought to be horsewhipped for letting you look into that den of vermin after your experience with the copperhead. I should have known better."

"Boy, am I glad I don't have to look at that snake in the jar any longer, but do you think Sly will believe me without the evidence?"

"Kit told me she's going to preserve it for you and keep it with her other specimen collection in case you ever need it."

"What wonderful friends. There's never a dull minute when you go there."

"I take it Kit didn't tell you they're selling out and moving across the state line," Dad said hesitantly.

"Oh, no," I said, hardly audible. "What awful news. When will they be going?"

"Not until next spring. With what they make on this property, they'll be able to buy a thousand acres further west."

"Will we still be able to visit them?"

"Of course. Just not as often."

****

They say that bad luck comes in threes. The third thing I broke nearly ticked Mom off again, not that I would have blamed her. It happened the night I promised Chappy I'd meet him at the

Open House Dance at the clubhouse. I admit I was giving the

supper dishes a lick and a promise when the everyday milk pitcher

slipped out of my hands and crashed into a zillion pieces all over the

linoleum floor. That seemed like a poor time for Mom to tell me

that it was a rare German antique, passed down from my great

grandfather's generation. I would have welcomed a thrashing with

the fly swatter to the three interminable days of silence I got.

Because we had no telephone, Chappy presumed I stood him

up. I wrote him an apology, and, being the sweet person he was, he

wrote back to tell me that he understood. Mim also jotted me a note

to say that 3D (our code for David Devlin Dwyer) brought Peg, a

girl from the city, and they spent most of the evening out on a bench

by the high dive smoking cigarettes.

I knew Mim meant well, but the image she painted hurt just

the same. I blew on my I.D. bracelet and shined it on my shirt.

Toby lay under the picnic table next to my bare feet. I rubbed his

back with my toes. "I'm never going to take this off," I told him,

"cross my heart and hope to die."

**\*\*\*\***

My streak of bad luck had ended by the time the Club held its last Open House of the season, which got me out of solitary confinement. I was nervous when 3D cut in on Chappy and me. He leaned down to put his chin on the top of my head, but I pulled away and asked him if he thought the Brooklyn Dodgers would win the pennant. I didn't want to get close enough to get a whiff of whatever it was that attracted me so.

"I see you're wearing your bracelet," he said, ignoring my question.

Before I could think of an answer that wouldn't have been a lie, Chappy tapped David on the shoulder and cut in.

****

For the balance of the summer I was stingy with the amount of time I was willing to share with my friends away from Toby. I rationed it like they did butter and gasoline during the war. I did spend one day canoeing with Mim on the lake and another trying to master the game she called *tennis*.

But just as that day in May when I wanted to put a chock behind the sun to keep it from setting, so now I was powerless to make summer mark time.  As daylight hours dwindled, the nights got chillier, making you pull for the covers.  Dependable nature put on her umpteenth perennial extravaganza, a splash that rivaled the niftiest fireworks display on any Fourth of July.  Generous and practical, she also gave Toby a thick winter coat, which served a double purpose, protection and warmth.  His color was as drab as a pile of dead brush.

Hunting season came, but Toby's size kept him from being fair game, although I breathed easier when the week-long shooting match was over.  There was no guarantee that the city slicker who shot my dog, Buddy, for a bear last season wasn't lurking around ready to take a pot shot at anything moving.

It was hard to resist the temptation to keep Toby in the chicken run, but Sly was a frequent visitor, searching hunters' pockets for slugs and fining violators heavily.

"If it's your job to protect animals, why won't you let me confine Toby for one lousy week?" I had argued.  "Hunting deer isn't like going fishing, where if you catch one that's too small, you throw it back.  When you shoot a deer, it usually dies."

Dad had overheard me and reprimanded me for being sassy to Sly, making me say that I was sorry for my outburst.

Mim, on the other hand, was pleased as punch that I'd squared off with Sly. "You're finally coming out of your shell," she said approvingly the next day at school.

The petition signed by over one hundred students making Toby our official mascot didn't impress Sly one iota. In desperation, as keeper of the evidence again, in case I needed it, I produced the pickled snake, but nothing I did satisfied his obsession.

Toby with silver bells

# 9

# **Heaven Sent**

Between hunting season and Christmas, Sly stayed away. Maybe he was busy making presents, too. Dad and I made Mom a Yule log out of a piece of white birch and decorated it with evergreens, holly and three red candles. Dad's gift, a pair of hand-knit hunting sox, was also a joint effort. I did the easy, straightaway sections while Mom did the tricky business of turning the heels and shaping the toes.

Toby was next on my list. He was a real puzzler, but finally, I settled on the idea of making him another tie, this one a wide, soft blue satin ribbon with tiny silver bells sewn on it that jingled softly. I was tickled to death to see that he liked it even better than his black bow tie. For some reason it made him silly, and he kicked up his heels like a bucking bronco, his little flag standing straight up in back. I got some adorable pictures for my photo album, my Christmas present from Mom and Dad.

A ripsnorter of a winter is how Dad labeled it. The blizzard started after Christmas dinner and didn't let up for three solid days. We were snowbound for two weeks, with twelve-foot drifts clogging the road in places where the wind whipped across the open fields. We shoveled and re-shoveled paths to the barn to tend the animals.

Toby was as snug as a bug in a rug under the newly-built lean-to. I made sure of that. Since school was closed my time was my own, so I stayed out with him until I got chilled to the bone and the feeling left my fingers and toes. Then I went into the house to thaw out, sticking my feet in the oven for a while.

"The way I see it, Tish," said Dad, rubbing his cracked hands above the stove lid to warm them, "one good turn deserves another. We had a bumper crop of apples this year. Those drops in the cellar will probably spoil before spring, so I think we should feed them to the deer.   If we don't, a good many of them will starve."

"That's awful," I said, thinking of Toby's mother and twin.

"Toby's fortunate that you've taken him under your wing. Not too many his size will survive."

After I got bundled up again, I took the flashlight and groped around our dingy, dirt cellar, stumbling over sacks of potatoes and onions until I located the bushel basket of spotted apples.   I transferred them to a burlap bag to make the carry easier.

Their normal feeding ground was the broad meadow beyond the mill at the foot of the mountain.   A stonewall capped with crusty snow divided the stretch equally, making a perfect, natural windbreak.   Besides the apples I carted a tarp full of hay.   Under ordinary circumstances, they would have turned their noses up at it, but since they were direly in need of food, I knew they wouldn't be fussy.

I stopped by the lean-to to tell Toby I'd keep an eye out for his family and then went in to defrost.   At first everyone thought I looked like the picture of health, with the flush of the great outdoors reddening my face, but Mom got suspicious when I put three kitchen chairs together and fell asleep before supper was on the table. When she felt my head, she knew that I was burning up with fever.

Dad brought down the small bed from the extra room and put it in the kitchen, which was the only room that was heated. They stoked the fire with coal to keep it burning all night. When the niter failed to bring down my temperature and I heard Dad say he was going for the doctor, I knew I was really sick.

I dozed on and off, conscious of the soggy towels on my forehead and the strong smell of rubbing alcohol in the room, but when a chickadee hit the kitchen window with a thud, I bolted upright. I knew the superstition. It meant that somebody was going to die. Although I wasn't as superstitious as my mother, I was feeling so deathly ill that it scared the daylights out of me. I thought I was a goner when Mom let Toby in to lay at the bottom of my bed.

Seven hours after Dad left, he returned on foot with Dr. Skinner, having abandoned the truck in a snowdrift three miles down the road.

When I opened my eyes the following morning, Mom, Dad

and Dr. Skinner were drinking coffee in silence. I tried to say good morning, but my throat was so sore I couldn't talk. I tapped Dr. Skinner on the back and waved my fingers.

"She's going to be all right," he said, a look of satisfaction on his face.

"Thank God," said Mom, rushing to help me untangle myself from the topsy-turvy covers. "You were delirious and thrashed about so, Tish, that Toby threw in the towel about midnight and went to get some sleep in his own bed."

I smiled. Dad and the doctor continued their conversation.

"Wes, that child's got the most diseased tonsils I've ever seen, and they've got to come out."

"But they've been put there for a reason," Dad argued, "and if you take them out, what then?"

"Ouch!" I managed to blurt out as I turned on my left side.

"The doctor gave you a shot of eh…"

"Penicillin, a new drug."

"If this agrees with you, Tish, Dad said, "no more horse tablets."

I grinned feebly, thinking of those enormous sulfa pills.

****

The medicine worked wonders, and in five days I was feeling fit as a fiddle.   The sad part was that as soon as I was up and about, Toby lost the privilege of being my bed buddy.   No amount of pleading could sway Mom once she'd made up her mind.   I even went so far as to credit him with my miraculous recovery, but Mom insisted it was the penicillin, the cod liver oil and the homemade chicken soup.

****

After I regained my strength, Toby and I resumed our daily treks after school and on weekends.   Of all the trees and plants in the woods, only the evergreens survived autumn's seasonal undressing, standing out like roosters in a henhouse of plucked chickens.   Snow still clung stubbornly to some bare branches like a temporary filling, but it took spring to bring everything back to life.

That's what farming was all about, new growth and new life. Even replenishing a flock of chickens with a brood of baby chicks was a blessed event, believe it or not.   When the weather moderated enough for me to shed my winter coat and go to school wearing a sweater instead, I knew it was time.

I balanced myself on the edge of the seat clutching four books and my lunch box, ready to dart for the door the second the bus came to a stop by the gas pump. I prided myself on knowing exactly where we were, even with my eyes closed. Elmer shifted into second and gave her the gas.

"Please, God, don't let us get stuck in the mud today," I whispered. "Mom gave me her word this morning that we'd go to the hatchery today."

"Armstrong farm," Elmer announced, looking at me through his rear-view mirror.

"Bye," I said. "See you Monday." As I picked my way from stone to stone up the driveway, trying not to get my loafers wet in the slush, I noticed the Chevy parked by the house. Bursting into the kitchen, I threw my belongings into the Morris chair beside the window. Mom wasn't wearing her apron, so I knew we were going to town.

"You don't have to change your clothes until we get back,

Tish," Mom said, shaking down the ashes in the stove. "I made you a snack to eat in the car."

"Yippee!" I howled, twirling my index finger like a lasso. "The red-letter day is here at last. I've got to go tell Toby. I'll be back in a jiffy."

"Not so fast, young lady. Why didn't you wear your arctics today? Do you want to get down sick again?" (I swear Mom had the eye of an eagle.)

They looked old-fashioned, and I felt like a drip, but I wore them grudgingly. I munched on my peanut butter and jelly sandwich all the way to the hatchery.

The chicks were boxed and ready for us in no time. I'd noticed a tinge of nervous excitement in Mom's voice too, as if she'd ordered a ticket to see "Gone with the Wind".

"Four dozen Rhode Island Reds?" Mom asked, double-checking the number.

"A baker's dozen this week, Mrs. Armstrong," the man replied. "You get fifty-two instead of forty-eight."

"Well, thank you very much," Mom replied, paying him.

I rode backwards all the way home, hanging over the front seat to watch the fuzzy little yellow peeping balls of down through the air holes in the lids.

Dad had already moved the wood box from behind the kitchen stove onto the porch so we could keep the chicks where it was warm. They would stay there until they were big enough to go into the brooder. Mim was flabbergasted when I told her we were keeping baby chicks in the kitchen. She said at her house that would be a definite no-no, because it simply wasn't sanitary. I reminded her that living on a farm was a far cry from living in a fancy house like hers.

"It's not fair," she told me at school. "You have all the luck."

By the time the brood feathered, I had chosen two to tame. Thinking they were roosters, I named them Dickey and Mickey. They were privileged chicks, roosting in Toby's old box on the screened porch. Every night when we came in from milking, the spoiled pair would be sitting by the door waiting for me to put them to bed.

It wasn't long, though, before they outgrew the box, and Dad finally gave me the word. "Tish, it's time they roosted in the coop with the other chickens."

"You're right, Dad," I agreed and carried my pets up to the hen house. It was dark inside, but I consoled them as I placed each one on a separate perch.

Before going to bed, Dad always went outside to check the sky. He could predict the weather with the accuracy of William Tell. "Tish," I heard him call. "I thought I told you to put Dickey and Mickey in the hen house."

"But I *did, Dad.* Honest." I went outside to see for myself. There they sat, huddled together, waiting to be put to bed.

Dad smiled and said, "Try again tomorrow night, Tish."

*The Easter hat*

## 10

## No Place Like Home

With all the catching up I had to do at school, before I turned around the slush turned to mud and anxious daffodils, pushing aside the remnants of last year's soggy blanket of leaves, stretched and yawned, nodding gracefully in the warmish spring breeze. Purple and white hyacinths sweetened the air, and forsythia blooms camouflaged the ugliness of the chicken wire fence.

For once my Easter hat didn't have flowers on it. I was much too old for that. It was straw-colored with a rolled-up brim and had a band of navy grosgrain ribbon, which hung down my back the length of my hair.

Since Mim's parents took us to Paradise Park, in return, mine had promised Mim and me a trip to see the Christmas Show at Radio City Music Hall in New York City, but the blizzard and my dumb sore throat put the kibosh on that. Instead, we made plans to see the Easter show, which according to Mim, was just as spectacular. She stayed overnight so we could get an early start the next morning.

Before bed, over Mom's objections, Mim set my hair in rag curls, and I heated the curling iron in the lamp's chimney to make ringlets for her. Foolishly, we spent a good deal of the night whispering about boys, Toby and baby chicks, so needless to say, we weren't exactly bright eyed and bushy tailed when the alarm jangled at 6:30 a.m.

"Sleeping on rag curls is torture. Remind me *never* to do it again," I grumbled to Mim. "It's like sleeping on a pillow of rocking chair rungs."

"We'll feel more human once we get all dolled up. Just think, this time next year we'll be wearing nylons and lipstick."

"I can't wait."

"Neither can I."

"I feel like such a dope in these little white anklets. Egads!" I gasped, studying my reflection in the mirror. Half of my hair was still tied up in knots, but the other half hung loose and straggly. "I can't go to New York City looking like this." Turning to confront the culprit, I began to laugh. Hers was nothing but frizz. She pushed me out of the way.

"Oh, good grief! I knew I should have left well enough alone."

"You look like a kissin' cousin to a porcupine," I giggled, hiding a grin with my hand.

"It looks more like I got struck by lightning," said Mim in her own inimitable way. "You should talk. It looks like you got your head stuck in the clothes wringer."

"Oh, that does it," I shot back, starting a pillow fight.

Wasting time on that left no time for vanity, so good old reliable braids were a lifesaver for me. Lucky Mim., her close-cropped hair was a snap to return to normal. A dousing in the washbasin restored its springy natural curl. Since we didn't want to start the day off on the wrong foot by missing the eight o'clock bus from town, we decided not to make a rumpus.

"You mind your p's and q's today, Toby," I said, giving him his orders. "And stay out of trouble. I'll be home before supper." I hugged him and Dad and we were off. Dad was sorry he couldn't go with us, but he was at a crucial place in building his fireplace and needed to lay the stone through the cut in the roof before it rained.

Kit met us at the bus stop as planned. The Warwick Stage was crowded with mostly men, well-dressed men reading morning newspapers. Mom and Kit found single seats near the front. Mim and I moved to the rear, hoping to find two together.

"Horsefeathers," I grumbled, disappointed that we had to split up. We plopped into the only two seats left, which were about six rows apart. Mom watched us until we were settled and then sat back to enjoy her day's outing.

In less than three minutes Mim sweet-talked her fellow passenger into trading places so she could sit by the window. Mine didn't take the hint but stared non-stop at her own reflection in the window, moistening her ruby lips and blotting them in three-quarter time with the tip of her pinky. She disposed of the excess by smearing it on her already rosy cheeks, rubbing it in, like liniment, in an even, counterclockwise, swirling motion. (Boy, Miss Wilson would give her an A in penmanship.)

About half way to New York she pulled a bottle of goodness knows what out of her purse. I *do* know that it smelled to high heaven, sickeningly sweet, like a patch of honeysuckle, lilacs and gardenias all growing together. She dabbed it liberally on any exposed area. "Want some, honey?" she asked, jabbing it in my direction.

"No, thank you," I replied, pretending to sneeze so I could cover my nose with my handkerchief. Being able to hold my breath for long periods of time was a godsend, and when I *did* inhale, I did so through my mouth. As we crossed the George Washington Bridge, although I tried desperately to fight it, I felt bilious. Perspiration dampened my bangs and my tummy did flip-flops. "Do you mind if we open the window?" I asked, forcing myself to be an extravert.

"It'll muss my hair, dearie," she replied with a pout.

"Here, you take my seat," I offered generously. "The wind doesn't bother me." Seeing she didn't budge, I had to play my ace. "I bet he's a swell guy," I said, flashing a momentary, Ipana® smile.

"How did you know I was meeting someone?"

I winked. "If you sit on the aisle, you can be one of the first ones off the bus."

She moved but none too soon. I opened the window, putting my nose to the air like Buddy used to do before he got shot.

**** 

When we regrouped in the terminal, Mom noticed that I looked a little peaked, but I sloughed it off and put on a good front, not wanting to put a damper on everybody's day.

Once outside, Kit suggested we take a crosstown bus. The thought of more motion and smelly fumes almost made me upchuck right then and there. "Won't we see more of the city if we walk?" I asked, swallowing hard, not letting on how woozy I really felt. "Remember, this is a first for me."

"Please," Mim whined, "let's walk."

Mom and Kit led the way. Mim and I followed. "You

look ghastly, pal, like you've been wrung through a knothole. What happened to you on that bus?"

"Please, don't even mention the word. You'd never believe it if I told you."

We walked east a few blocks, then north. Yet, instead of acting like a hick from the sticks, gawking at the skyscrapers, I behaved like a kid from the city, oblivious of the wonders around me: 42$^{nd}$ Street, the Time Life Building and Rockefeller Center. Concentrating on getting my sea legs, I missed it all.

Kit knew the city like the back of her hand. "There's a donut shop up ahead," she said, turning around. "We've got time. We'll stop for coffee."

That did it. I'd made donuts. They swam around in hot, bubbly oil. "Ugh!" People and places swerved and faded in slow motion as I weaved in a stupor, futilely trying to keep my balance and stay on my feet. While Mim screamed, Mom and Kit reacted, catching me and dragging me into a nearby drugstore. I sat with my head between my knees until the room stopped spinning. Someone shoved some foul-smelling stuff under my nose. I pushed it away. Pretty soon I felt normal and sat up. "Wow! That was a weird sensation," I said to Mim, who looked almost as white as her hat. She was speechless for the second time in her life.

Against Mom's better judgment but upon my insistence, we went to the show. I felt so-so. Our seats were ideal, dead center, about halfway down. I sat on the aisle, then Mom, Kit and Mim. The glorious Easter music played on the magnificent organ I'd waited so long to hear gave me goose pimples. I tried so hard to enjoy the performance, to ignore the rumbling in my stomach, but from past experience, I knew it was only a matter of time before I lost my cookies.

Since I wanted to leave as quickly and inconspicuously as possible, I got up and made a mad dash for the rear of the theater. Toby and Star had nothing on me now. I knew exactly what it was like to chew the cud. Mom scurried up the aisle abreast of me with Kit at her heels. When Mom saw I wasn't going to make it to the rest room, she took off my new straw hat with the navy-blue grosgrain ribbon and held it in front of me. Although it spared the spongy, red carpet, my Easter hat ended up in the garbage can.

Naturally, Mom wanted to stay with me, but Kit wouldn't hear of it. "I've seen the orchestra rise up out of the floor skatty-eight times," she argued. "You haven't."

In the corner of the lady's room stood one of the biggest scales I'd ever seen. It was as tall as my Dad, with a three-foot square weighing platform on the bottom. The huge, clock-face dial at the top made the good-sized railroad clock at our train station look like a peanut.

Thanks to the kindly attendant, this is where I sat for the next three hours--on and off--so to speak. Surer than shootin', I didn't gain any weight; if anything, I lost a few pounds. Kit sat on the scale beside me, her sneakers noticeably clean and her slacks noticeable creased. "I didn't get to tell you our news," she said cheerfully, trying to get my mind off my misery. "We finally sold the farm and bought a two thousand-acre spread in Pennsylvania."

"Dad told me," I said weakly. "I'm happy for you and Henry, but we will miss you so much."

"Bless your heart," she said, patting my hand.

"Tell me all about it," I said with a sickly smile.

"Picture this, Tish," she said as if she was describing her wedding dress. "A thousand acres of prime timber:   hickory, hemlock and white pine, an apple orchard, a dandy trout stream and a three-acre pond."

"And a house and barn?" I added in a questioning tone.

"How could I forget.   A big, white house with three guest rooms, one reserved for you and Mim whenever you want to come."

"How long will it take us to get there?"

"About five hours, give or take a bit."

"Yipes.   I've never gone that far from home before."

Kit smiled her ready smile, smoothing my bedraggled bangs with her stubby, rough hand.   "It'll be another first."

****

Getting me home was a nightmare I'd like to forget.   Did I say *I*?   Mom and Kit made a seat by crisscrossing their arms and carried me to a waiting taxicab.   It wasn't like Mom to splurge like this.   "We'll get you back home by hook or by crook," she said in a determined voice.

The Warwick Stage was nearly empty, so we all sat together

in the front. When we got as far as Paterson, I knew it was no use.
I wasn't going to make it by bus. I was as limp as a wet dishrag.
The three of us got off while Mom continued on to bring back the
car.

****

The maddening thing about the whole sorry mess was that
the minute I got home, I felt fine. Nobody said a word when I
poured the perfume out of my atomizer behind the wood shed.

Although I looked like death warmed over for a week or so,
the color gradually returned to my cheeks, and in no time at all, they
were as pink as the petals on the bleeding heart.

Mim and I went into fits of laughter every time we thought
of the fate of my Easter hat.

"What's so funny?" Artie asked one day at recess.

"It's a private joke," Mim and I said together, hooking
pinkies and making a wish.

*Toby*

# 11

# The Patient Patient

Toby changed dramatically during the winter and early spring. His taste turned from cow's milk to bark, stripped indiscriminately from Dad's peach tree saplings, a development not appreciated in the least. He grew about a foot in stature but a yard in spunk. He was tall enough to eat Cherrios® off the kitchen table and ornery enough to openly show a dislike for Sly, unprompted by me, honest to engine.

His display of naughty behavior occurred shortly after he sprouted a miniature rack of velvet-covered antlers. He had walked me to the school bus and was minding his own business chomping on some clover at the edge of the cow pasture when Sly veered into our driveway. Without looking up from my book, I knew who it was by the knot that suddenly formed in my stomach. As the cab door slammed, I lowered my book for a second to view Toby's reaction. He stood motionless, like a taxidermist's specimen. "It's all right, pumpkin," I said soothingly. "Don't be afraid." He dislodged a persistent insect from his ear with one swift flicker and continued to eat.

To have a chance to win the school championship in today's spelling bee, I needed to get a few more troublesome words down pat, and I didn't need any distraction to interfere with my concentration. Turning my back to it, I leaned on the top bar rail, overlooking the tranquility of the pasture lot. "Rescind, r e s c i n d," I repeated over and over again, hoping that it would sink in by rote.

The scene before me was a picture no artist could paint, as Gram would say. Against a backdrop of shapely spruce and towering pine, a lone apple tree, like a giant nosegay, stole the scene. A sprinkling of buttercups and a few clumps of white daisies, tastefully placed, added the finishing touches. "T e n a c i o u s," I spelled, riveting the sequence of letters in my memory. "Oh, beans," I said. "If I don't know them now, I never will."

Unable to resist the temptation, I broke off a daisy. "David loves me. He loves me not. Loves me. Loves me not. Loves..."

"HELP!" Sly yelled. "Somebody call him off."

I spun around to see Toby in the stance of a billy goat holding Sly at bay against his truck. Mom, Dad and I converged on them from different directions, but I got there first. "You little nincompoop," I whispered, steering him a safe distance away. "You've got us in Dutch now, mark my word. "Sly's as mad as a hornet on a piece of fly paper."

"He went berserk, I tell you," Sly bellowed at Dad. "It's all *her* fault. She's responsible," he accused angrily, pointing his finger at me. "She sicked him on me."

"That's nonsense, Sly, and you know it. An animal senses who his friends are, and, evidently, you're not one of Toby's favorite people. He's just feeling his oats a mite, that's all," said Dad, the peacemaker, coming to my defense.

Elmer honked and I ran for the bus, leaving Toby in Mom's capable hands. He trotted down to see me off, as he did every morning and Mom followed.

"Hello, Toby," the kids all called, leaning out of the windows.

Sly took advantage of the diversion to crawl back into his cocoon.

I slumped in my seat, pretending to study the unnatural sky all the way to school. Through my tears it had a bruised look, similar in color to the black and blue marks I got when I fell off my bike.

"Sly was scared out of his wits," I told my friends. "You'd think Toby was a sixteen-point stag instead of a harmless, little squirt."

"You're absolutely right, Tish," said Chappy. "As it stands now Toby is cute and no threat to anyone. But he won't stay young and innocent forever. You're going to have to face that fact sooner or later. Then you are going to have to make a very difficult decision."

"The thought has crossed my mind," I said, wandering off away from the group to be alone.

****

I needed a breather, a brief interlude where nothing traumatic happened, but it wasn't in the cards. The following Saturday morning Mom's shouts awakened me.

"Shoo. Shoo. Skidoo. Go away, Toby. Go away."

"You little imp," I said to myself, "what deviltry have you been up to already today? It must be serious. Mom sounds awfully perturbed." I made it to the back door in record time but then stood at the brink as though I'd been starched from head to toe.

Mom flailed her broom at Toby, whisking him off the step. Unaccustomed to such ill-treatment, he tilted his head and looked up at her in bewilderment. "You're dripping blood all over the walk. Oh, what's the use," she said to him in exasperation. "Heavens to Betsy, I'm talking to a deer. I think I'm ready for Morris Plains."

"I'll clean it up," I said, coming out of my trance.

"Before it gets tracked all over my clean kitchen floor," she cautioned, the irksome note leaving her voice.

I stooped down stiffly to examine him, still in a state of shock. He looked so pathetic. Blood oozed from jagged tears in the velvet on his tiny antlers and dripped down his face. "For Pete's sake, Toby," I said painfully, "it looks like you got mangled in a meat grinder. How on earth did you ever hurt yourself like this? Have you been scuffling with another deer?" I questioned harshly, wiping the salty tears from my mouth on the sleeve of my pajamas.

Dad came from the barn to see what all the commotion was about.

"Toby's hurt," I cried, scrutinizing the extent of his injuries. "Don't let him out of your sight, Dad," I begged. "I'll be back pronto." Not waiting for his answer, I ran into the house to get some medicinal supplies. Since we had no bathroom, the medicine cabinet was in the kitchen. "Iodine. No. That stings," I said, making a snap judgment. "I'll use mercurochrome instead. And Watkin's salve. That's good. After accumulating the necessary bandages, adhesive tape and scissors, I hurried back outside to dress

Toby's wounds.

He was a good little soldier, never flinching as I picked and poked, trying to mend the tattered covering. I worked intently, but bandaging the skinny spikes was easier said than done.

"Look up, Tish," said Mom. As I did, I heard a click. I was so absorbed in giving Toby first aid that I hadn't noticed Mom poised to take a picture a short distance away.

"There, that should do it," I said with satisfaction as I fastened the last strip of adhesive tape. "They'll heal in no time, won't they Dad?" Mom stood silently by taking this all in.

"I told you that Red Cross course you took would come in handy someday," Dad replied, neatly sidestepping the question. "I'll tell you what. Why don't we take the day off and go hiking up to the Tory Caves? I've been meaning to remark that trail all spring."

Mom stepped forward then and put her arm around me. "You won't hear that offer again in a month of Sundays, Tish. If I were you, I'd take him up on it."

"What about Toby and his injuries?"

"He's going to be fine.  Believe me."

****

Dad was at home in the woods, more so than in the house. He started out working for a big industrial company when he was sixteen but soon quit, because he couldn't stand being cooped up all the time indoors.  In the valley he had the reputation of being built like Paul Bunyan and having the strength of Hercules.  He could barrel through a thicket like a deer and climb a side hill like a mountain goat.  I was breathless trying to keep pace with him.

Of course, Toby didn't let us go without him.  He was like a kid at a county fair, straying off to sample one of everything-- partridgeberry, trillium, spicebush, and wintergreen.  He was no trouble to spot.  His bandages stood out like a white shirt in a St. Patrick's Day parade.

Dad's hearty laugh ricocheted off a rock ledge.

"What's so funny?" I hollered, catching up to him.

"Can you imagine, Tish, what those city slickers would do if they came along and saw a deer with his antlers all bandaged?"

"They'd hightail it out of here like scared jack rabbits."

"Swearing they'd seen a ghost," Dad concluded, chuckling like somebody was tickling his ribs.

I was too worried about Toby to appreciate the humor in it, and to be truthful, I was surprised and a little jarred at Dad for taking Toby's misfortune with a grain of salt.

Dad notched the last tree at the end of the trail, a sturdy white ash, and I wondered if we'd blazed the same path as taken by the Tories over a hundred and seventy years before. "I wonder if they were ever sorry they left America, Dad?"

"It must have been a heartbreaking decision in many instances. Families were split up, even our own governor's. But once they made the choice and sided with the British, they had no alternative. Those who stayed were ridiculed, tarred and feathered or burned out. As far as I know, the folks who hid in these caves fled to Nova Scotia. Governor Franklin was arrested and jailed in Connecticut and eventually went into exile in England, never to be reconciled with his famous father, Benjamin.

"After we eat let's explore the caves to see if we can find a relic to donate to a museum."

"Good idea, young lady. I don't know about you, but I've worked up a whopper of an appetite."

"Me, too." I unpacked the knapsack and spread everything out on a large, flat rock. Mom had outdone herself and prepared a small feast: gobs of cold chicken, biscuits, her homemade bread-and-butter pickles, chocolate cake and a thermos of hot tea. The apple, I figured, was intended for Toby.

"What a day to be alive," Dad said, leaning against a tree trunk sipping tea and chewing on a toothpick. A fluffy cloud mass glided overhead like a stealthy Zeppelin in flight.

"It's a humdinger," I said, agreeing. The food, fresh air and physical exercise combined to knock me for a loop, and I had all I could do to ward off a sleepy spell. To stay awake, I got out one of the flashlights and aimed its beams into the recesses of the cave. A rustling noise sent me scurrying back to Dad's side in a hurry. "There's something in there. I heard it," I said under my breath.

"Could be an animal hibernating. I tell you what we're going to do," he said calmly, taking the other flashlight and motioning for me to follow him.

We scaled the mound of earth and stone with the grace of two bobcats and lay face down on the mossy ground when we reached the top. We inched our way over the edge as far as we dared. I felt like a possum hanging from a clothesline. I copied Dad's lead and scanned the inside with the broad beam of light.

"There's a family in that cave all right," Dad said as he focused on six pair of glittery eyes.

"Ah, how adorable," I said softly purring like a contented kitten. "But I thought raccoons nested in tree hollows."

"They do, but oftentimes they're lucky enough to find a cavern like this for a nursery. Come on," Dad said, clicking off his light, "we're intruding. She's got her hands full as it is. We can explore another cave."

Toby normally ranged about making his own fun but usually kept within earshot of me. When Dad and I returned to our picnic spot, he was nowhere in sight, so I gave him a call.

"Baby raccoons are as cute as a bug's ear," said Dad

"Yeah, especially their little black masks and ringed tails," I answered, gabbing away a mile a minute. "Toby," I called again, "where are you, you little rapscallion?"

"For cryin' out loud, Tish, leave the poor thing be for five minutes. He can take care of himself. Don't be such a worrywart," he said, tossing me a scoop.

"I'm sorry," I said, "but it just isn't like him not to come when I call him."

There were no surprise cave dwellers in the second one; in fact, there were no relics either. It was as clean as a whistle. "I give up," I told Dad at last, losing patience with the project.

"Go find him," Dad said, sensing what was on my mind.

I stepped outside, batting my eyes until they adjusted to the bright sunlight. A shift in the breeze rustled the trees and whipped the clouds into stiff peaks, like a bowl of beaten egg whites. Shading my eyes against the glare, I called and called, but my voice didn't carry and was lost in the wind.

Thinking he might have gotten bored and had gone home on his own, I started running down the trail, stumbling over rocks and swinging at switch-like branches that swatted me in the face. A tree root tripped me up, and I sprawled face down on the ground panting.

I lay for a few seconds wondering whether I was all in one piece.

I heard a scuffle of feet behind me and rolled over half-expecting to see Dad. Springing up like a jack-in-the-box, I threw my arms around Toby's neck. Stunned, I suddenly realized that he had not only rid himself of his bandages but had also scrapped all the velvet off his little antlers, his first set of horns, and they were *magnificent*!

"He's as proud as a peacock," said Dad, who was standing a stone's throw away with his thumbs hooked around the buckles of his overalls, not missing a trick.

"You knew, didn't you?"

"I had an inkling."

"Then why did you let me make a fool of myself this morning by bandaging his antlers?"

"Because sometimes it's better to learn things this way."

*Graduation day*

## 12

# Doomsday

May, the month whose job it is to grow the flowers watered by April showers, turned out to be a real wet blanket. The sky was so gray that I thought the earth was smoldering, belching puffs of sooty smoke, which formed a dull and uninteresting canopy overhead. An occasional thundersquall erupted to water down the soup, but as soon as it blew through, the fog thickened again.

People visited a lot to break up the monotony. Uncle Wally brought Newton to see Toby one Sunday afternoon. Mom asked him why Minerva didn't come too.

"I tried to convince her that the safest place to be during a storm is in a car, but she insists it's under a bed with a pillow over her head, a bed with *metal* springs, mind you," he said, getting a good laugh from Newt and me.

In a way, though, the foul weather was my salvation, since it kept me indoors quite a bit. It gave me time to memorize "The Polonaise" and to finish hemming my graduation dress. Toby's routine was discombobulated, too, but he took it in stride, foraging between drops and then returning to the lean-to to chew his cud during storms.

Part of getting ready for graduation was learning not to say the word 'ain't'. It was hard to believe that *nobody* in high school used the word, but that's what Miss Putnam, our eighth-grade teacher told us. I took particular notice at home when my parents said 'ain't' to see if it grated on my eardrums like Miss Putman said it would and darned it if didn't! Mim .and I corrected each other constantly trying to break the habit, scared stiff that we'd sound like kids from the sticks. After a while it rubbed off on Mom and Dad, too, converting them.    In time, the majority of people in the valley followed suit, casting it out like a rotten apple.

June made up for May by giving us powder blue skies and warm, dry days.    Toby and I had waited patiently for the weather to clear.    That's why I wasn't overjoyed when I got a letter from Mrs. Kelly asking me to work the entire weekend.    "What a mell of a hess," I complained to Dad, sounding like a real sourpuss.

"Bad news?" Dad asked, seeing the open envelope in my hand.

"No.   Change of plans.   Uncle Bob offered to let me use his rowboat on the lake.   He said it was good and sturdy and had a wide, flat bottom.   I was looking forward to giving Toby his first ride, but now I've got to work."   I read him the letter.

"Bob has been hounding me to take the boat out and troll for bass.   I'd be happy to take Toby with me for a spin.   You two have the whole summer ahead of you for boating."

"You're tops, Dad," I said, brightening.

**** 

After being closed up all winter, the house smelled musty.

Mrs. Kelly and I threw open all the windows and gave it a good airing. We made up beds, washed windows and floors, dusted and vacuumed. The Hoover beat our carpet sweeper by a mile. When Mom and I did our housecleaning, we had to take up our rugs, hang them over the clothesline and beat them to death to loosen any deep-seated dirt.

After supper Mrs. Kelly and I were kapooed and went down to sit on the dock to watch the sunset. The afterglow had all the colors of a ripened peach, and its reflection bathed us in a mellow tone. A dozen canoes effortlessly skimmed the smooth water. Mim was probably in one of them. I hadn't had time to write to let her know I was coming to the lake. My chair squeaked as I strained myself forward trying to pick her out.

"Why don't you call Mim tonight," said Mrs. Kelly, not even opening her eyes.

"Thank you," I said. "It'll surprise the stuffing out of her, since we don't have a telephone at home."

"Tish!" a familiar voice called. "I thought it was you. Hello, Mrs. Kelly."

"David. Hello. Good to see you."

"Does Tish have time for a ride? He paddled alongside and got out, holding the line in his hand.

"I'm not leaving until tomorrow," I said, finding my voice.

"Then, hop in."

"I'm really too tired."

"Here, David, take my seat. I'm going up to the house," said Mrs. Kelly. "Toodleoo, young people."

"Thank you," he replied, smiling. "And welcome back."

David looked wonderful. He had grown inches and had shaved off the fuzz over his upper lip. After tying the canoe fast, he sat on the wooden planks facing me. We exhausted our common and separate interests, talking easily and comfortably, like we used to, like there was no lapse of time.

"Tish," he said, reaching out and taking my hand to keep me from picking at my nails, "I like you a lot."

"I know," I whispered, "but the worlds we live in are too different."

"My parents think so." He stood up and turned away,

looking over the water. "They've taken me out of the public high school. I'll be going to a private school this fall."

"That means you'll definitely be going to college, you lucky duck. You must be *very* excited. I got up and turned him to face me. I turned up the corners of his mouth into a smile.

"It'll be a new experience," he replied, returning to his old jovial self. "What about you?"

"I guess I'm going to be a secretary."

"Not a teacher? What happened to *that* idea?" he asked, twisting my silver bracelet to show the signet.

"Afraid not. I've got to go in," I said.

"Yeah. I have to shove off, too."

I stood on my tiptoes, and he kissed me goodbye.

The afterglow had vanished when David steered his canoe across the lake, leaving my world a forget-me-not blue. I waved in his direction, but he was blurry and out of focus, because my eyes were so full of tears.

****

The balance of the month was a whirl of activities. Chappy

took me to the eighth-grade dance (as friends). Graduation day came, but my dress still had a few straight pins in it here and there. I told Mim if the Amish could do it, why couldn't I? (kidding, of course).

Like all the others before us, our graduation ceremony was very moving and beautiful. First, we sang "America the Beautiful". Then we did our choral reading:

'By the shores of Gichegumy, by the shining big sea waters, stood the wigwam of Nacomus....'

Next on the program were the eighth and seventh-grade choruses singing "The Bells of Saint Mary's" in harmony. It was so beautiful that I got chills.

After the applause died down, Miss Putman said, "And now we shall hear Letitia Armstrong on the piano. She will play Chopin's "Polonaise". At the risk of sounding swell-headed, I must admit that I did a bang-up job, even though I did skip a whole page. Maybe it was because there was someone in the audience I was trying to impress. I received a thunderous applause and even a few bravos.

The finale was stupendous as always, with the flower girls and boys, overladen with bouquets and baskets of peonies, roses and whatever else our gardens provided, wending their way up the aisle through the honor guard of garland bearers to the waiting graduates. It was a night to stamp into your memory.

After the recessional, the Dwyer's fell all over me, wanting to know where in the world I learned to play like that.

I've been studying piano for the last six years," I answered politely, excusing myself to find Mom and Dad.

I congratulated Mim, but she hugged me cautiously, not wanting to get stabbed. Her chief concern was whether her seams were straight or her lipstick smeared.

"Yes and no, you loony tune," I said affectionately.

"3-D's heading this way. He's home from school already" she announced out of the side of her mouth. "I'll catch you later."

David made his way through the crowd and kissed me on the cheek. "I didn't know you were a famous virtuoso.

I blushed. "Do you like classical music?"

"Did you hear the bravos?"

*Tish by the field corn*

# 13

# The Ultimatum

The thrill of graduating lingered in my mind throughout the summer. I felt like I'd reached my first plateau. The second one loomed large before me, challenging yet frightening, because I didn't know what to expect.

Toby continued to delight and astonish visitors, especially Fr. Barry. One Sunday afternoon after church, Mom and Dad invited him in for tea and cake. Since Mom was in a congenial mood, she didn't object when Toby came in, too. Nothing fazed

Fr. Barry. He was used to our menagerie, but when my deer leaped over a kitchen chair as gracefully as a horse bounds over a wall, I thought his eyeballs would fall right out of their sockets.

The following Friday as I sat on the split-rail fence reading a letter from Mim, laughing like a hyena, Hank, the reporter I thought I'd never see hide nor hair of, showed up to do the story on us.

"You've caught me at a bad time," I gasped, trying to talk with no breath left in me. "Forgive me for being so giddy, but I can't help it." I continued to laugh until I cried and my sides ached. "It's no use," I said, wilting like a frostbitten petunia. It was infectious, and he began to roar also not even knowing why. "Oh, I finally said, "I just can't laugh anymore."

"What are we killing ourselves over anyhow?" he asked, wiping his eyes.

"Well, my girlfriend is a sleepwalker. Guess where her mother found her." I hadn't even delivered the punch line, but the two of us were cracking up all over again.

"I have no idea," he said, catching a breath. "Where did she find her?"

"Sleeping in the *bathtub*--with her pillow and all the covers!"

Even after he got down to brass tacks and started taking down material for his article, Hank had to chuckle every once in a while.

Toby and Mickey and Dickey had become best friends, and I was happy that he got some precious pictures of the three of them eating together. This may seem like a trifling tidbit, but Mickey was king of the walk in the chicken run, and when he strutted his feathers, the other chickens scattered. Toby and Dickey were the only two who weren't intimidated. Since spring, Mickey had grown giant spurs and was tall and proud, with shiny, golden plumage and a fine, red comb and wattle. What's more, he had learned to crow. On the other hand, Dickey had grown plump and cinnamon-colored, and to my chagrin, *he* began to lay eggs!

It got a few laughs, not half as many as my Easter hat, though. When Mim came on her two-week vacation and I told her the news, she said she was from Missouri and had to see for herself.

After that, Dickey never had a minute's peace, with Mim trailing her like a bloodhound. Between you and me, I think Dickey gave in and laid an egg on her day off just to roust Mim out of the hen house.

Oddly enough, the two special events happened simultaneously. I converged on her, laughing like a ninny, tossing my copy of the *Town Ledger* high above my head. Although Hank had wrapped it round and round with twine, it had loosened, and the raw edges caught the breeze, twirling it back at me like a homemade handkerchief parachute. Mim, on the other hand, came jigging across the lawn like a person who'd just won the Irish Sweepstakes clutching her fragile prize, a single, little brown beauty. She carefully deposited it in Dickey's own egg carton before she turned her attention to me and my news.

"Toby made the front page," I shouted, almost pushing the screen door off its hinges.

"Hurry up slowpoke," she prodded. "Let's see. Let's see."

"Just a darned minute, Mim," I said, sliding a hot peach pie to the far end of the table before spreading out the newspaper.

"Patience, girls, patience," said Mom, peering over my other shoulder. "Ut oh," she sighed, drawing in a sharp breath and biting her bottom lip. "I think we're in trouble if Sly sees this."

"Henry, you dunce!" Mim exclaimed, banging her fist on the table.

"Don't blame Hank," I said dejectedly. "It's all my fault, but he was so close to them when he took that picture that I never dreamed the fence and the gate would be in the background. What a sap I am!"

"I'm afraid I can't argue with that, my friend," Mim said, drumming her fingernails on the porcelain-topped table.

"What's done is done," Mom said resignedly. "Stop fretting and be glad that Toby's gotten the publicity. Maybe somebody in authority will read it and change the law."

"How jerky can we get?" Mim said, attacking the table again and jiggling the kerosene lamp. "I've got a brainstorm. Here we are stewing and worrying about whether Sly will see Toby's picture taken in the chicken run when he probably doesn't even get the *Town Ledger*."

I sat rigid and dry-eyed, hearing nothing but the pounding of my heart in my ears. After finishing the article, I rose from the chair like a zombie, detached and empty, and left the house.

"Wait up," Mim cried, loping after me. Toby joined the chase as though he were 'it' in a game of tag.

I took the shortcut through the meadow, that was now glutted with goldenrod. In an adjoining pasture the cows, mooing softly, gathered under the apple tree, their bags puffy with evening milk.

I lunged headlong into the woods at the edge of the clearing, galloping down the crunchy path that led to the brook. Crossing over it to the pine tree on the opposite bank was a cinch, since there was only a trickle of water flowing over the rocks. A flock of starlings, rising in one, black mass from the surrounding evergreens, soared eastward in perfect formation, reminding me of the days when squadrons of Corsair and P-38 fighters zipped across the sky heading for the war zone. Any other day I would have enjoyed the birds' chirruping, but today I was happy we flushed them out, grateful for the unusual stillness. I needed to hear myself think.

Mim understood my need for solitude and kept Toby amused while I wrestled with my painful decision alone. However dreadful, it had to be made.

"My heart aches for you, Tish, she said, unable to control the quiver in her voice after I confided my plan to her.

"There's no other way."

The pallid sky matched the tone of our sunken spirits as we trudged home like a couple of sad sacks, responding to the supper bell. The sound carried easily on the stagnant, motionless air. Toby stopped now and then to sniff it, his sensitive nostrils pulsating rhythmically. I followed his every precious movement, committing each one to memory.

I was sure he knew before we did that the green truck was in the yard. Sly hopped in it as we approached and banged the door shut. Mom lured Toby over to her by taking a shiny, red apple from her apron pocket and offering it to him. He took it like the gentleman that he was and carried the repast up to his bed under the lean-to.

"Yes, we'll see you the day after tomorrow," Dad said, cutting Sly short and seemingly taking the words out of his mouth. As he turned away to join us, Dad's face was unnaturally pinched and pained. Of course, I had heard the remark and knew Sly was coming to take Toby away.

Mom and Dad understood when Mim and I asked to eat our stew with Toby and didn't object when we wanted to rig up a place to sleep there.

"As long as you're careful with the lantern, I guess there's no harm in it," Dad said, smoothing his mustache with his thumb and forefinger. "I'll check in on you when I come out to determine the weather for tomorrow."

I took three cushions and gave Mim the mattress from the glider. If I got too comfortable, I'd never hear Mickey crow at five o'clock, and we didn't dare risk using an alarm. We played Parcheesi for a while, but our hearts weren't in it, so we quit after bed check and lay looking at the sky. There was a ring around the moon, a sign that the drought might be over.

I slept in fits and spurts and was wide awake long before dawn seeped over the horizon, hoisting its red warning flag. Mom always said, 'Red in the morning, sailors' warning'. "Mim," I called softly, ignoring the threat, "it's time to go."

"Brrr," she said, wrapping up in her quilt. "What happened to summer? Look, I can see my breath."

"Here, put this on. It's an old mackinaw of Dad's I found hanging on a nail in the barn."

"What'll you wear?"

"Once we start moving, I'll be fine."

The temperature had nose-dived during the night, and the ground, warm from days of baking in the hot sun, reacted to the cold moist air much like our lungs did, expelling steam. The lantern cast an eerie shadow over the field of fleeing ghosts, and as we progressed single file, with Toby bringing up the rear, Mim pressed closer and closer, tripping over my heels.

An acre of field corn twelve feet high gobbled us up for the next while, its oversized leaves paddy whacking us as we hurried through the mill. On the other side at last, we doused the light and hid the lantern. I relieved Mim of our knapsack of provisions, strapping it on my back to help insulate me from the nippy breeze.

"What if a car comes?" questioned Mim, her teeth chattering.

"One won't," I replied confidently, plodding up the center of the road, bucking the wind with every step. The mile seemed like ten, but like a captain guiding his ship into a snug harbor, I steered my tiny band into a familiar wood lane where we were not torn to pieces by the crummy old wind.

"I've got a pain in my side," Mim complained, hobbling up to me.

"I'm sorry," I said. "We can slow down a bit now, but I want to get back home before we're missed."

"And before it rains," Mim added, pointing upward.

A body of smokey-colored clouds separated us from the warm rays of the August sun just as an unthinking hunter hogs a wood stove blocking the heat.

"Tish," Mim said, rubbing her stitch, "it might just be wishful thinking expecting Toby to find a mate and live happily ever after, free from *you* and Sly. Remember, he's only a yearling. Besides, such things only happen in the movies."

"Maybe so, Mim, but I've got to let him go. I've got to give him his freedom." I choked up and couldn't say another word.

"I understand," she said, knowing how hard I was straining inside to keep a stiff upper lip. "So, let's go. Can't you see I've got my second wind?"

She ran on ahead, but I saw her wipe the cuff of the old plaid mackinaw across her eyes. She was hurting too, because she loved Toby almost as much as I did.

Although Toby and I had never ventured as far as the deer run before, I knew every landmark from listening to years of hunters' yarns. "That oak," I told Mim, pointing to one with a butt as big around as a washtub, "is where one of those city slickers' dogs treed a coon one night, so the story goes. Well, they couldn't sight that little devil for love nor money, not even with a half dozen lanterns. He wasn't going to let a raccoon outsmart him, so he climbed the tree after it and got as far as that crotch when he let out a bloodcurdling yowl. He found his coon all right. I'll bet he's still got the teeth marks in his hand to prove it."

"Serves him right," said Mim.

Around the next bend a sheer, moss-covered cliff rose out of a garbage dump of enormous rocks. "Dad said they were probably deposited there during the glacial era about a million years ago."

"What a sight!"

Toby led us to the path. It angled down the far side of the mountain, outlined the rock pile and snaked through the underbrush to the brook. By the number of fresh tracks that went every which way, we figured we'd picked a likely spot. After setting our bait, Mim and I crouched beside a boulder to watch and wait.

Toby wasn't bashful. He dug right in, eating his fill of cracked corn and then topping off his breakfast with a big, juicy apple. It suddenly dawned on me that Mim and I hadn't eaten a bite since last night's supper, but even if I'd brought something along, it would have been impossible to get a morsel past the lump in my throat.

Toby, suspecting nothing, probably thinking we were playing that silly game of hide-and-seek again, trotted down the winding path to the brook for a drink, not knowing that I was deserting him forever.

We stared at each other briefly, our fists clenched over our mouths to hold back the sobs. In no time we ran the return distance, heeding neither gusty winds, freezing cold, murky sky nor the approaching storm. Sick and tired of issuing warning after warning, it finally struck with a vengeance the minute we stepped foot on the main road, drenching us to the skin.

****

"I can explain," I said standing in the doorway, looking like a drowned rat. Telling Mom and Dad what we'd done and getting their blessing took a big load off my mind. I even felt tired and surprisingly hungry. After some hot tea and toast, believe it or not, Mim and I fell asleep sitting up, wrapped cozily before the fabulous fire in a couple of warm, woolen blankets.

By noontime the downpour had stopped, and the clouds gave way to splotches of blue. Mim and I weren't feeling very chipper yet, despite a nap, and had started a game of Monopoly$^©$ on the kitchen table. Her first time around she bought the Boardwalk, which usually made me mad, but today nothing could get my dander up.

An unwelcome draft entered as the door opened, and I nestled down, pulling the blanket over my head.

"Wes, please," Mom protested.    "Put the board in the hole. These girls are chilled to the bone."

"Tish," Dad said, shutting the door quickly behind him, "look who the cat dragged in!"

I threw off the blanket, hoping against hope that it was who I thought it was, sending red hotels, green houses and orange Chance cards helter-skelter.  Toby licked my salty tears as I clung to his neck, venting all my misery, anger and love.

I felt Dad's rough, gentle hand on my shoulder.  "Tish," he said, "it's a five-hour drive to Kit's.  You two had better get bundled up and get Toby ready to travel."

*Toby's first horns*

## 14

# Living

Although Labor Day was past, the bleached shades of summer lingered, along with the dust. Taking an ironed handkerchief from my pocketbook, I spread it neatly on the cement close to the orange gas pump and sat down. The bus wasn't late. I was early. On purpose. Anxious, I guess. Happy to be out of the hospital in time for the first day of school, overjoyed that my week's agonizing bout with infantile paralysis had not crippled my arm as the doctors had feared. I was lucky to be able to hold a pencil and write. That very day I began to recount, on paper, the wonderful experience I'd had raising Toby.

I didn't open the album now but worked from memory. Looking at his pictures still made me cry, and it would never do to get on the high school bus with red, puffy eyes.

All too soon I saw the yellow bus jouncing across the flat, churning the road's powdery surface into a cocoa-colored tornado. It was time to tuck my memories away and let a brand-new experience fill my life. But I missed Toby waiting beside me. The kids did too. I could see them craning their necks, wondering where he was.

# Afterword

My autobiographical novel is a heartwarming story, chronicling the unforgettable childhood experience I had raising an abandoned baby fawn.

Most of it is true. Although the warden's obsession to put Toby in a preserve is real, his mannerisms and speech are strictly figments of my imagination, likewise, the man at the train depot. The event at Uncle Wally's never happened, and the two farmers are fictitious also. I added it to demonstrate my Dad's phenomenal agility; however, the slaughtering of the one hundred chickens actually happened years later when our puppy and an accomplice had a field day littering the ground with our neighbor's six-week-old pullets. Mim (name change) was my closest friend in grammar school. We did spend a lot of time together, but at her house, not mine. The focus had to remain the farm locale to move the story to its conclusion.